IMP

A Political Fantasia

Politics as *Un*usual!

Thomas P. Powell's ascension in politics was both unusual and yet very American. From traffic cop to Vice President of the United States, his climb up the ladder of public service was often due to the push of random acts and not-so-happy accidents—although Thomas held the opinion that it was due solely to his singular innate moral authority. What matters is what's within; that's the Powell political philosophy. Then, on the cusp of his grasping the last rung on the American political ladder, something truly within suddenly appears. A horrible homunculus, an impetuous imp, climbs out of Thomas's right ear to bedevil his nights, confuse his days, and take him on a crazy, wild, nauseating, and nuclear journey.

It's *The West Wing*
as if done as an episode of
The Twilight Zone

ADVANCE PRAISE FOR IMP

"Steven Paul Leiva is a very bad man. His version of U.S. politics Trumps anything the real world has to offer. Hell, you thought the orange one was the only homunculus America had to worry about? You thought wrong. There's always the nuclear option." — **Steven Savile,** *New York Times & USA Today* **Bestselling Author.**

"Steven Paul Leiva is a master wordsmith able to take on any genre or blend them, as in the case of *IMP, A Political Fantasia.* Once started, I couldn't stop reading. The tale was just long enough yet had me longing to read more of Leiva's prose." *Zoommmmbizzt!* I highly recommend this novel. — **Jean Rabe,** *USA Today* **Bestselling Author.**

PRAISE FOR OTHER "WILD TRIP NOVELS" FROM STEVEN PAUL LEIVA

TRAVELING IN SPACE

"Many of the aliens' encounters with human beings are downright funny...much to think about, and I'm sure that *Traveling in Space* will play on my mind for some time to come" — **Russell Blackford, Author of *Science Fiction and the Moral Imagination.***

"A deadpan, laugh-out-loud look at first contact told from the alien POV (with aliens that are as messed up as the rest of us). Recommended!" — **Stephen Webb, Physicist, Author of *If the Universe Is Teeming with Aliens ... WHERE IS EVERYBODY?: Seventy-Five Solutions to the Fermi Paradox and the Problem of Extraterrestrial Life.***

THE DEFINITION OF LUCK OR THE POST-MODERN PROMETHEUS

"Having a special appeal to readers with an interest in philosophy and science fiction, *The Definition of Luck: Or The Post-Modern Prometheus* showcases author Steven Paul Leiva's genuine and impressive flair for originality and the kind of narrative-driven storytelling that fully engages the reader from beginning to end. Thoughtful, thought-provoking, original and entertaining...unreservedly recommended"— *Midwest Book Review*

"What I can say is this is a very well-written book. Yes, it is Science Fiction and has some interesting ideas, but the description of the friendship between Astro and Neuro is the core subject of this book. Once you realize this, it puts things into perspective, which is probably why I've continued to enjoy thinking about the book long after reading it. 'The Definition Of Luck Or The Post-Modern Prometheus' certainly gets a recommendation from me." — **Andy Whitaker**, *SFcrowsnest*

CREATURE FEATURE: A HORRID COMEDY

"*Creature Feature* is a weird, funny, twisty romp through the creepier parts of the American landscape. Highly entertaining and highly recommended." — **Jonathan Maberry, New York Times Bestselling Author of *Rot & Ruin* and *V-Wars*.**

"Viva, Vivacia! *Creature Feature* is a treat for everyone who grew up watching vintage sci-fi and monster movies on late-night TV presented by their favorite local horror host. This book tickled my funny bone while gnawing on it with razor-sharp fangs. As the Vampire Queen might say, it's ghoul-tastic!" — **Greg Cox, New York Times Bestselling Author.**

JOURNEY TO WHERE

"A deftly crafted, inherently interesting, and thoroughly entertaining read from cover to cover, *Journey to Where* impressively showcases author Steven Paul Leiva's genuine flair for originality and a distinctive, reader-engaging narrative storytelling style...unreservedly recommended."— *Midwest Book Review.*

"The author's true strength is in storytelling. The attention to detail is spot on, providing just enough visual imagery to fill the reader's perception without diluting the setting with unnecessary clutter. Throw this in with a strong cast and a nicely paced plot, and *Journey to Where* by Steven Paul Leiva is a fun read sure to entertain fans of the classics."— *Amazing Stories Magazine*

EXTRAORDINARY VOYAGES
Including the Novella Made on the Moon

"This brisk and touching comic novel has mysterious and profound things to say about the price of freedom, and it is not without relevance to the way new and disturbingly pernicious myths about freedom are being propagated every day in Trump's America. Highly recommended!"— **John Billingsley, "Dr. Phlox" on** *Star Trek Enterprise*

"With just enough satirical elements to emphasize the blurred line between logic and insanity, true fans of Science Fiction will find a kindred attachment with the Stanley Lewis character. *Made on the Moon* by Steven Paul Leiva shows us that reaching for the stars is not just a dream; for some, it is a way of life." —***Amazing Stories Magazine.***

A Political Fantasia

IMP

A POLITICAL FANTASIA

STEVEN PAUL LEIVA

Magpie

Press

Los Angeles, California

ISBN: 979-8-218-39683-1
Library of Congress Control Number: 2024906949

Cover Design by: Juan Padrón
https://www.juanjpadron.com/

Author Photo by Amanda Martin

Published in Los Angeles, California
Printed in the United States of America

FOR MY DAUGHTER NANETTE

MAY THE WORLD BECOME WORTHY OF HER

1

The thing that must be understood is that Thomas P. Powell was a very moral man. It was not a morality born from a sacred text or the values of a particular community or the admonitions of an authority figure. It was a morality that had been born with him and in him and was as natural to him as his beautiful and fine head of hair, which he had always paid just the proper amount of attention to.

It could easily be said that if any man knew right from wrong, that man was Thomas P. Powell, vice president of the United States of America.

And the knot in his tie was just not right.

With a sigh, he undid the knot and started over. He correctly positioned the thick end of the tie against the thin end and, after a centering breath, looped the tie, brought it around, and tucked it through with the grace and precision of a *ballerino* executing a leap to the expressed awe of an appreciative audience.

Done.

Perfect.

Thomas smiled the slightest of smiles, allowing himself just the minimum display of self-satisfaction.

"*Daaaadddyyy!!!*" Young vocal cords had sent out the call. It had no trouble traveling out of a room, down a hall, and into the second-floor turret room that was the bedroom of the vice president and his wife. It found Thomas standing in front of a full-length mirror.

"Yes, Charles?" Thomas answered, raising his voice to carry.

"*Can you come here? Maximan broke.*"

"Again? Well, bring it here."

"No! You come here!"

There was no reason not to. Thomas P. Powell was now fully dressed and was ready to leave his bedroom, and probably would have stopped off to say goodbye to his son anyway. So why did he expel a parental breath of frustration? Preparation for frustrations to come, perhaps?

Thomas found his son, Charles, six years old, dressed in a crisp and neat school uniform, sitting on the floor of his bedroom surrounded by a plethora of "Sold Separately" accouterments to his superhero Maximan action figure. There was the Maxicar, of course, and his Antigrav-propeller, which strapped to his back, and several energy pulse weapons that fitted over his arms, becoming powerful extensions to those appendages.

"Charles! Get off the floor. You'll get your uniform dirty. How often have I told you you do not play on the floor when you're in your school uniform?"

Thomas had respect for uniforms. He had once worn one. He had always kept it crisp and neat.

Charles stood up. "I'm sorry, Daddy."

"Now, what's the problem?"

"Maximan's arm came off." Charles held out his Maximan action figure in his right hand and its severed right arm in his left hand.

"Well, yes, Charles, if you continue to throw Maximan against the wall, that sort of thing will happen. Let me see it."

"Well, he has to fly." Charles handed over the damaged superhero.

"Not without control, Charles, and that control is you keeping him in hand and flying for him."

"It's not the same."

"No, it is not; I understand that. But it is better and more practical if you don't want a broken toy. Now let me see…"

Thomas looked at the body and the appendage and saw where and how they could be brought back together, although not without some struggle—which was true of much more than just broken toys. After this assessment, Thomas set to work.

"Is all your homework done?"

"Yes."

"Everything placed neatly in your backpack?"

"Yes."

"Have you had breakfast?"

"Yes. Mom said I could play until she's ready."

"Well, yes—if all your duties are done."

"Mom says you shouldn't call them duties."

"What should I call them?"

"Chores."

"Chores then. Here you go." Thomas held out a fully recovered Maximan.

"No. You be Maximan, and I'll be Valquar!"

"Charles, I do not have time to play. You know this is the morning I have breakfast with the president."

"Uncle Georgie won't care if you're late."

"Charles, how often have I told you not to call the President of the United States 'Uncle Georgie'?"

"That's what he told me to call him."

"Fine. Are you going to listen to him or your father?"

"Well—he is the president, and you're only the—"

"Yes, well …"

"Just make Maximan shoot at Valquar, and Valquar will try to escape, but then he'll die."

"Okay—escape."

Charles ran around his room, flying the supervillain as Thomas aimed Maximan's right arm with the energy pulse weapon and said, "Bang! Bang! Bang!"

Charles stopped and turned to his father and gave him a look one would think quite beyond a six-year-old, but one that every parent has a secret fear is well-stocked in their child's arsenal. "Daaaadddyyy! Maximan's gun doesn't go like that. It goes *zoommmmbizzt!*"

"Charles, guns, in my experience, always go bang-bang-bang. We can only operate from our own experience. How often have I tried to tell you that?"

Thomas P. Powell knew what he was talking about. He had been a police officer in a small town in a rural community on the eastern side of the northern half of the state of California. He had been first in his class at the county police academy. He had taken his training, the profession he was training for, and himself so seriously during his eighteen weeks at the academy that the other cadets began calling him Barney Fife. They did this to his face, assuming that calling him Barney Fife behind his back would do him no good. He was neither amused nor moved nor insulted by this, just saddened that the other cadets were spending more time watching ancient shows on cable TV and streaming services than they were attending to their studies. This nickname stuck with him as he joined his hometown police force and was assigned to traffic patrol. He wrote more moving violation tickets in his first year on the force than any other officer had in the seventy-five-year history of the town. And no officer had ever written as many tickets for the infraction of the failure to use a turn signal as Thomas P. Powell. Motorists who did not use their turn signal when required to—upon a turn right or left or changing lanes—irritated him greatly. He considered it one of the most visible—despite being non-visible—indications of the decline of civilization. For Thomas, it was not just a safety concern but a matter of common courtesy upon which civil society rested. And so when he saw a lane change, a turn right, or a turn left with no red light blinking, he set and locked his jaw as he threw the switch that would blare out the siren. He had developed a pertinent lecture to deliver to violators. It was short, not at all sweet, and made drivers feel not at all good about themselves. Whether his vigilance in this led to a diminution of this particular infraction of the traffic laws was never assessed as Thomas P. Powell's time on traffic patrol was cut short. His law enforcement career—of the utmost importance to him—was relatively short for such a good officer.

"Mr. Vice President, the car is here."

Secret Service agent Jeff Wolfe entered Charles's bedroom to make the announcement. He was a tall, reasonably attractive young man, the attractiveness centering on a smile that women looking for children and children looking for non-scary adults found welcoming.

"Hi, Jeff!" Charles said, delighted to see him.

"Hi, Charlie," Jeff answered, always happy to know that such a swell kid existed.

"Charles, I have to go," Thomas said.

"*Thomas!*" Another call traveled the hallway. This one came from Kathryn, the Second Lady of the Land.

"Yes?"

"*I need to see you before you go.*"

"The car is here."

"*Doesn't mean I don't need to see you.*"

"Right. Okay, I'll be right there." Thomas said as he handed Maximan to Jeff and started to leave, stopped momentarily by a shooting pain in his right jaw, which he attended to by opening his mouth into a vast stretch. He then continued to the accompaniment of:

"You can't get me, Maximan!"

"Don't count on it, Valquar! *Zoommmmbizzt!*"

Kathryn Powell was finishing dressing. It was a morning moment Thomas had always enjoyed witnessing. It was the culmination of a proper focus on freshness and fashion. The freshness of the body, renewed by sleep, bathing, and possibly some subtle scenting. And fashion to clothe the corporeal—a practical need, given climate fluctuations throughout the planet and the day and the fragility of our thin, nearly hairless hides. But it was also a very human statement announcing not only our presence but also our ascendance. Even without an official designation, what each person wore each day and night was a uniform, and each uniform was coded, and each code was so helpful in a social structure. Or so Thomas felt.

Kathryn Powell had always been good at wearing the proper uniform. Even when he first met her when she was new to his hometown and starting a job at the public library. It was not a well-paid job, and yet she always looked properly the professional guardian of books. Not stuffy or fussy or prim, as many years past might have seen in a librarian, but respectful of her position, of the fact that she represented to the public all the books on the shelves and all the wisdom contained therein. But also the bright joy, the hard facts, the sloppy sentiments, the chuckles and guffaws, the awe, the tension, the mystery, the suspense, the horror, and the satisfaction of resolutions. Thomas had been incredibly impressed.

And now she stood there "outfitted" correctly for the wife of the Vice President of the United States in a black skirt, cream-colored blouse, and lightly lavender jacket. They would see her through a day of meetings, a speaking engagement, and helping out later at Charlie's school. Her day's activities would be covered by official government photographers and a press corps a bit larger than was normal for a VP's wife. But she was beautiful in her thirties, and the camera loved her. And so the press, who relied on the camera, loved her. She was quite aware of those facts, but only as facts to note and utilize, not as attributes to take credit for.

She was a wonder. That's what Thomas thought. As a beautiful woman with a striking personality, she was a wonder. He would often gaze upon her when her gaze was diverted. It brought him immense pleasure.

Kathryn would have been delighted to have known this. She may have suspected it, but to know it for a fact would have been nice. But it was not the sort of thing Thomas felt needed to be expressed. Or, possibly, he couldn't find the words to express it. Or, if he could have found the words, possibly he never found the proper moment—or the proper courage—to express it.

Kathryn turned to Thomas as he entered, "I'm sorry, but I really do need to talk to you."

"Oh, that's okay. I don't want to go anyway," Thomas said, walking over to their bed and sitting down. "I hate these breakfasts."

Kathryn looked down on Thomas and wondered why he had to say such things. "Thomas, most people would love a weekly private breakfast with the President of the United States."

"Most people don't know what an old bore he is."

"He is not an old bore. George Knight is one of the most delightful gentlemen to have graced that office."

That was President Knight's reputation. It was the common wisdom in DC, in the press, across America. But Thomas P. Powell knew better, as he had often tried to explain to Kathryn. "He's an ineffectual, weak leader! I don't want to go through this argument again, Kathryn. I try to talk policy to the man, and he wants to talk to me about—" Stop. Leave it alone. It will only mean ...

"About what, Thomas?"

"Well, about—you and Charles and the family and—you know, my pain."

"What pain?"

"You know, this TMJ jaw thing I've got." Thomas massaged the spot on his right jaw to alleviate the pain—and generate some sympathy. It was ineffective in both cases.

"Oh, you should stop grinding your teeth when you sleep."

"Yes, thank you, Kathryn, good advice. Unfortunately, I'm asleep at the time I'm asleep, so I'm not likely to be aware of it, am I?"

"My dad went to the dentist and got this plastic mouth insert to stop the grinding."

"Yes, I know as you, and he told me about ten dozen times."

"And yet, you still don't go to the dentist."

"I don't want to put something in my mouth when I sleep. It's too weird."

"It's practical."

"It's weird—and somehow unseemly."

"Unseemly? You think it's unseemly?"

Thomas thought it would be unseemly to answer this question. "He keeps trying to be my friend."

"Who?"

"The president."

"It used to be that vice presidents complained that their presidents ignored them. Count yourself lucky to be VP in a new era."

"You're reading the president the wrong way. This is no Bill and Al partnership or Obama and Biden. And it's certainly not George and Dick—or should I say Dick and George? Knight gives me plenty to do, but he's never given me any real power."

"Your time will come."

"You're damn right it will."

"Assuming you treat your president with a little more deference so that you can get his endorsement."

"Oh, he'll endorse me all right."

"Why?"

"Because he knows I'm the best man for the job. Who else in the party or the opposition has my intelligence, my story? I don't want to get into this destiny argument with you again; you have your beliefs, and I have mine."

Kathryn walked over to Thomas. "Yes, let's not get into *that* argument again." She took his chin, lifted his head, and sweetly kissed his lips, which Thomas accepted and appreciated while wondering if it had been a dismissive gesture. Then Kathryn, still holding his chin, pulled back to get a good view of his face, which she studied briefly. "You need more lines. You don't have enough lines in your face to be president. Your youthful demeanor, while making you devastatingly attractive, especially when you smile, which you don't do enough, would be detrimental in negotiations with world leaders and the Congress."

"So, you think I should smile a lot to crease my face? Ow!" The TMJ flared.

"Or grimace your face in pain; that could do it too. I see your secret strategy now. I prefer the smiles, though."

Thomas smiled. It hurt. "Now—why did you call me in here?"

"I need you to ask the president something for me today."

"Kathryn, I do not like being a messenger boy."

"Thomas, this is important. The president asked me to oversee the Literacy in America program. I think I'm doing a good job. But I need his help. I need for him to appear at the conference in April."

"There are channels to go through. Have your office call—"

"Thomas, if I go through channels, I will never get to him, and you know it. Please remind him today that the Literacy Conference is coming up and that it would be a big boost if he would give the keynote address. Now the First Lady agrees with me that—"

"Then why doesn't the First Lady ask him?"

"Because she feels it would be better if you ask him. I think she still feels a bit intimidated by him."

"Understandable. Being thirty-five years his junior and all."

"Yes, she's still basically a kid. She never expected to be First Lady."

"Well, that was not too bright of her?"

"Thomas, I will not hear one word against Sarah Knight. She's helped bring a fresh new spirit to this country. She's an amazing woman."

"Yeah, yeah."

"Now go say goodbye to Charlie."

"I already have. We played."

"Really?"

"I was inadequate with the sound effects, but other than that, I guess we had fun."

"I'm pleased."

"Good—your pleasure has always had a high placement on my agenda. Right up there with campaign finance reform."

It was not an ironic statement. Thomas was perfectly sincere. But it also did not sound like an affectionate statement, so Kathryn tilted her head and gave him a crooked smile of guarded thanks. "You better hurry. The president awaits!"

Thomas left his residence and was greeted by his driver holding open the back door to his official limousine. It was by now quite a usual scene, and yet, this morning, something was missing.

"Where's Agent Wolfe?"

8

"I'm sorry, Mr. Vice President. He went in to get you, Sir, and that's the last I've seen of him."

Then, descending from the heavens, the answer arrived.

"*Zoommmmbizzt!*"

"Ah, yes …" Thomas said to the heavens.

"Do you want me to go get him, Sir?"

"No, I will. I can say goodbye to Charles again. But please call the White House and tell them I'm running late."

As he walked down the hallway to Charles's bedroom, the great battle was coming to its conclusion.

"*I got you now, Valquar!*" Maximan proclaimed triumphantly.

"*No! No!*" The villain said between giggles.

"*And now you must pay the price of your evil—tickling!*"

Thomas found his Secret Service agent and his son on the carpeted floor of the bedroom, Charles down on his back, Jeff hovering over him and showing him no mercy as he tickled his tummy. Charlie was lost in laughter. Neither were aware of Thomas.

Thomas watched and listened and took it all in. Then he set his face hard and said:

"Excuse me, Agent Wolfe. I don't mean to break into playtime, but I am running late for a meeting with the Leader of the Free World."

Alerted and alarmed, Agent Wolfe rushed to get up on his feet. As he did his sidearm, a SIG Sauer P229, as blunt and ugly a weapon as had ever existed, fell out of his shoulder holster and landed on the thick carpet before Charles.

"Oh, cool!" The young boy said as he reached—

"Charles! Don't touch that!" His father shouted louder than the son had heard him shout before. Charles froze.

Jeff scooped up his weapon and holstered it quickly. "It's okay, Sir. The safety was on."

Thomas scooped up his son and started to vigorously brush off his school uniform, making it clean again; making it neat again, confusing Charlie, who thought he was possibly being spanked.

"It's not okay! Charles, I don't ever want to see you reach toward a gun again. Your little playthings may go zoom-zit-burt—or whatever—but that gun really does go Bang! Bang! Bang! And it can kill you!"

Charlie's eyes widened in fright, filled with tears, but Thomas did not notice.

"Sir."

"What?"

"Charlie." Jeff's voice was deep with concern and forced Thomas to look, taking in Charlie's face, full of fear and questions he did not know how to ask. "Oh," Thomas said as he collapsed to envelop his son in a hug. He whispered into Charles's ear. "It's okay. I'm not mad. Time to be a man."

Time for whom?

Thomas stood up and recovered himself.

Jeff felt a deep need to apologize. "Sir, I—"

"It's over, Agent Wolfe. Let's go."

Guns go, Bang! Bang! Bang! Thomas P. Powell knew this intimately. Not just because he had had weapons training and continuing practice as a police officer but because he had seen a young, angry man shoot and blast away the red flesh of his old high school coach, Mr. Anderson, a tough son-of-a-bitch, but fragile when it came to bullets. Thomas had been off duty, visiting Mr. Anderson, as he often did, as they shared a world view. The young, angry man, a junior, an Internet nut, had had it with being invisible and walked down the school hall methodically looking for particular persons who would die. Then, it would be time for the rest in a wholesale action. Mr. Anderson was the first one he saw, which pleased him, as Mr. Anderson had been at the top of his list. A bullet also hit Thomas in the arm, knocking him to the ground as the young, angry man traveled on, screams were heard, and crying started.

There was so much wrong with this. Thomas was angry over so much wrong. He got up and pursued the young man. He was not armed; his new wife did not like him to carry a weapon when he was off duty. It had been a mistake to accommodate her. He found the angry young man. He told him to stop. He told him he was wrong. He told him in a scream so loud and insane that the angry young man fell back to being the confused and shy non-entity he was used to being and not the center of all existence that the gun had placed him in. Thomas slapped that gun from his hands then slapped the angry young man, then knocked him to the ground. The angry young man had not had time to shoot anyone else.

Thomas was declared a hero. Thomas became famous. Thomas entered the national stage. Thomas's life changed.

Thomas came to see the incident—although he never revealed this to anyone, not even his wife—as evidence of his natural moral authority.

President George Knight was a sixty-six-year-old man who inspired old-fashioned words when colleagues and the press and then—following suit as they always do—the people tried to describe him. *Gentleman* was one of those words, as was *avuncular*. Although few knew why or what it referenced, *Solon* was often used. And that rarest of descriptions (as the object described had become quite rare), *statesman,* had been applied to him, although many thought it should have been reserved for his obituary and his eulogy. Oddly, *philosopher* was never used, despite him looking like one, with his shock of wavy, white hair and a face that had always looked wiser than that recent familiar visage among professional politicians: *wiseass.* If anyone had been tempted, they would have been discouraged in a most determined manner. No politician wanted to be seen as a philosopher, for most Americans felt most philosophers should be neither seen nor—God forbid!—heard. Wise like a beloved uncle or a country gentleman close to the land (a near-mythical but still appealing creature) was fine. As was any wisdom as long as it was deemed "common." But a philosopher? No. Heads in Washington should never be in the clouds—so common wisdom said.

Once a week, President Knight had breakfast with his vice president, a man he had barely known when he had plucked him out of the House of Representatives. Thomas P. Powell had been in his second term (the first of which he had been appointed to) as the congressman from a large and square (in shape) district holding a sparse population. He was young, good-looking, telegenic, and a sort of a "war" hero. The party liked him, and the president could find no real objections to him. He had undoubtedly not wanted any of his peers from his generation of politicians who would every day feel that they had had enough of a history with him that they could challenge him. The president did not mind being challenged, such is politics, but he did want a vice president young enough to deal with the disappointment when his challenge was rebuffed.

The breakfasts were often an ordeal. Policy would be touched on, but only touched on, disappointing Thomas. Chitchat, gossip, and personal news could have filled the time in a personable manner, all of which the president had relied upon throughout his career. But Thomas had always found such small talk unreliable and was poorly practiced in them. So, between sips of coffee and ingesting an excellent American breakfast, there were often long silences that the president usually had to end.

"How were your eggs," the president asked Thomas.

"Fine, Sir, fine," Thomas said, addressing more the eggs than the president.

"Done exactly to your satisfaction?"

"Yes, I believe they were," Thomas said, having to think about it because he now had no memory of having eaten the eggs. But he must have, for there it was before him, his plate, empty of eggs. "Yes, they were fine."

"Good," the president said with a slight smile. "Because last time when they weren't and—"

"I did apologize to the chef, Mr. President—as you requested."

"Good ... How is the family?"

"Fine, Sir. Fine. Everybody's fine. And the First Lady, and the, uh, the twins?"

The president beamed, looking just like many photographs of himself. "First rate! Sarah, you know, has worked very hard to help them find their separate identities despite being identical twins. But we had our first crisis in this regard the other day when I managed to get some time away to join them on a little shopping trip."

And photo op, Thomas rather cynically thought.

"You see, both girls fell in love with *exactly* the same outfit. Now, Sarah has never dressed the girls alike—despite pressure," the president leaned into Thomas to state this State secret, "from the White House communications office—but the girls both wanted this outfit. Sarah suggested tossing a coin; I suggested arm wrestling. The girls would not hear of it; they simply wouldn't. They both wanted that dress! So, for the first time, Sarah reluctantly gave in. We got home, and the girls rushed to their room, put on their new dresses, and fixed each other's hair in the exact same braids, which is pretty amazing for six-year-olds. Then they came to us in the family room. They were so cute we couldn't believe it! So, Sarah has thrown up her hands to biology, and she's looking online for matching outfits for the girls." The president paused and sipped coffee, warm, not hot. He raised his hand, and one of the White House waiters came over. "A hot pot, please, Darren."

"Right away, Mr. President." Darren, a tall, elegant man who had served many presidents, grabbed the white porcelain coffee carafe decorated with the Presidential seal. Thomas truly loved that carafe.

"You know," the president continued, "it's amazing to be going through these experiences at my time of life."

"Yes, I can imagine." Thomas tried to keep the irony out of his voice but did not fully succeed. For he could not, indeed did not, want to imagine. He had always found older men with young wives unseemly, bordering on the absurd. It was much too much the "throwing up of hands to biology" for Thomas. The older men were usually rich or powerful, not that there was much difference between the two, and so such marriages were clichés as well as being unseemly—so typical, so, so—expected in a very elite way. Not to mention the insult to past-their-prime women. Not that Thomas would ever say his opinion to the president.

But he did want to say…

"Sir, um, I was wondering, now that the midterm elections are over, when are you planning to announce your plans for another term? Assuming that you are going to run."

"Interesting that you should ask that question."

"Is it?"

"As you know, I retired from the Senate when Sarah and I married. I figured thirty years of service to the good people of Delaware was enough. I had a new, young, shall I say, fresh wife, and I was looking forward to spending some, um, 'quality' time with her at our place on the Brandywine River. And when I wasn't with her, I could research Revolutionary War battles like I've always wanted."

"Well, you certainly would have deserved the retirement, Sir. Your record in the Senate was brilliant."

"Thank you."

"I was surprised when you accepted the VP position on the ticket."

"Thomas, when your party and country call you to serve …"

"Often people refuse the call—especially lately."

"Yes, you're right. That was a self-serving statement. Henry wanted me on the ticket because I was the least controversial person he could find—fair enough. I also knew that with him as president, the vice presidency would amount to semi-retirement, if not retirement itself.

Henry didn't like partners. So, I figured four, maybe eight years of easy, ceremonial service to my country; then my lecture fees would quadruple. I saw it as enhanced social security for my new family."

Darren brought in the fresh, hot pot of coffee and poured a cup for the president and one for Thomas. The president took an appreciative sip, then said, "Never thought Henry would have to resign three years into his first term."

"Bringing considerable shame to our party and this country," Thomas declared as if he had been the only one to see this and, more importantly, to be offended by it.

"True," the president said, expressing only a factual acknowledgment. "My motto has always been, 'Be rosy with donors, but never be cozy with them.' But you, Thomas, have done an incredible job reversing that shame by your work on campaign finance reform. You've helped push a masterful piece of legislation through Congress."

Thomas had not expected the compliment, as deserved as it was. And so, with some surprise and sincere appreciation, he said, "Thank you, Sir."

"Of course, it's going to make it a bitch for us to campaign effectively in the next election."

Thomas did not take this as a compliment. "So, you are...?"

"Yep! I'm going to run. I'm having too much fun!"

Fun? Whee! and Yaaa! and Woo-who! in the Oval Office? "Excuse me, Sir, but is service as president of the United States an occasion for fun?"

"Thomas, Harry Truman had fun, Richard Nixon did not. Can you read the lesson in that? Besides, you're not ready to be president."

Thomas hated his mind being read, hated being at all transparent. But what was, was, and had to be dealt with. "I see. May I ask why you would hold such an opinion?"

"Because, Thomas, your ass is so tight it's a wonder you can take a dump."

Thomas P. Powell had always prided himself on what the common man might call his poker face, but what he considered an admirable control of his emotions. Not that Thomas felt anything was wrong with emotions—it was just that other people tended to play upon them to their advantage, which he thought was a pernicious violation of one's self. So, he had worked hard not to let his face become a beacon of his feelings. In this instance, though, of the president of the United States, the leader of the free world, the defender of "capitalism" and "free enterprise," informing him of a possible rectum-based rectitude, his face failed him.

"I see you have been accused of this before," the president said, and with just the slightest of smiles, he drowned in his cup of coffee.

"I am who I am, Sir. I conduct myself in the manner that I believe is proper."

"Thomas, you are one of the most moral and upright men I have ever met. It's shocking that you come from California."

"Well, my family's been there for four generations."

"Yes, I think that may well be part of the problem. You had no 'West' to escape to. So, it all backed up. You're intelligent and talented, Thomas. But you have the empathy and tolerance and just plain human connectedness of a fucking Iranian Ayatollah."

"Sir, I—"

"Don't argue with me. I'm giving you the blunt end of my wisdom. And don't think I don't know your real opinion of me. But I am still the president of the United States, and I will be so—God and the electorate willing—for the next six years. If you want a shot at the eight following that, you have to do one thing for me. You have to give up some time over the holidays."

"For what?"

"Before our new surgeon general joined the administration, she used to do seminars for major corporations in empathy heightening. She has graciously agreed to conduct a three-day seminar for some of my top-level people at Camp David this weekend. I want you to attend it."

"Oh, no, Sir, please! I'm not good in such situations like that."

"I know, that is why I want you to attend it. The Interior, Commerce, Transportation, and Labor secretaries are all going."

"And the secretaries of State, Defense, and the Treasury?"

"Oh, they are far too busy."

"And I'm not?"

"It will be private, fully secure, and without publicity."

"But —"

"Do this for your president, Thomas; do this for your country; do this for yourself," the president commanded.

Thomas pushed his chair back and stood up, "Yes, Sir." There was nothing else left to do but leave.

"Oh, and Thomas ..."

"Yes, Sir?"

"Give my regards to Kathryn, and please tell her I will be happy to speak at the Literacy Conference."

"Oh, yes, I meant to bring that up."

A beautiful woman walked into the dining room. One of those exceptional women whose beauty was far more than mere surface details, although the surface details were all quite remarkable. She was a totality of admirable attributes and seemed in her being to be proper or correct or flawless or perfect or befitting. And yet, there was a slight aura of fragility about her. It may have been her relative youth. It may have been that she did not believe that she was proper or correct or flawless or perfect or befitting. But it was most likely just some small wrong that only brought greater attention to all that was right.

"Lucky for you," the president said to Thomas as he stood up to greet his wife, "the First Lady mentioned it to me."

A kiss was exchanged between this man and his wife, a long, affectionate, slightly teasing kiss. Thomas found it off-putting.

"Ah—yes—thank you, Sarah," Thomas said to the First Lady. "You have saved me an argument at home."

Sarah Knight left the lips of her husband and turned to Thomas, giving him a big, bright, and warm smile. "Don't mention it. I'm a strong supporter of domestic tranquility."

"Well, goodbye, then." Thomas turned to leave and was almost knocked over by two bolts of raucous energy as Lisa and Molly Knight, in matching outfits, ran into the room and jumped into their father's arms.

2

Richard D. (Ricky) Newberg, the tall, elegant ex-governor of Nevada, now the Secretary of Transportation, sat in a fat, comfortable, floral-pattern chair and cried. He was dressed in jeans, a Western-style shirt, and boots. He blew his nose into a red bandanna.

Oh, please, thought Thomas, who sat in another fat, comfortable, floral-pattern chair in the living room of the Aspen Lodge at Camp David. He was leaning back in the chair, almost as if to put as much space between him and the tearful transportation tsar as possible.

The other cabinet members all sat on the edge of their seats as if, at any moment, they would reach out to Ricky to touch or hug or, at the very least, caress him with their deeply sympathetic eyes.

Around the square, dark wood coffee table sat Lawrence "Larry" Stern of Virginia, the Secretary of Interior, his exterior covered in a tee-shirt from the Shenandoah National Park and a pair of green Dockers; Mildred "Muffie" Miller from Connecticut, the Secretary of Commerce, in a lavender running outfit; Robert "Bobby" Franklin, the Secretary of Labor, in sweatshirt and shorts; and the Surgeon General of the United States, Mary Scott Momaday, a full-blood member of the Navajo Nation in Arizona, in some casual native wear that seemed, to Thomas, to "show off" its native authenticity rather too loudly. The vice president was dressed relatively casually—he had taken off his suit coat.

Larry, Muffie, and Bobby sat on a couch with no floral pattern, while General Momaday sat in the third fat, comfortable, floral-pattern chair.

"Ricky, that was an absolutely wonderful hurt. A fine hurt," the Surgeon General said in the soft, kind of arrogantly pleasant, breathy voice that Thomas had too often heard Native Americans use, a voice dripping with honeyed wisdom and damn self-satisfied about it.

"Thank you," Ricky said as he recovered himself.

"I am somewhat surprised you put that much emotional investment into a golf club."

"Women never understand," Ricky sobbed.

"All right, good point. I will try to work on that. I will try to understand. As I'm sure that Muffie will as well. Won't you, Muffie?"

"Uh, yes, of course," Muffie, a middle-aged woman, very fit, accomplished, and rich, said. "After all, *hurt is hurt.*"

"That's right, hurt is hurt. Once revealed, we must only extend our senses to the hurt, not to what caused it. This may be foreign to our experience; therefore, we can't understand it anyway, but the hurt is hurt. Hurt is universal. And hurt, we can understand. Now, hasn't this been great so far? Great catharsis! Great purging!"

There were nods of acknowledgment and, from Ricky, a long, slow, and juicy blow of his nose.

"Not to mention," Momaday mentioned, "a great way to clear sinus passages."

Secretarial-level laughter went around the room. There was, however, no vice-presidential laughter.

Thomas was quite aware of Momaday's accomplishments. From a small native school in a small native village to Harvard to Oxford to Johns Hopkins to country after country, researching not illness but health, finding the science behind native well-being, both physical and mental. Awards and honors had become almost native to her. As fine an individual *Homo sapiens* as America had ever produced. And yet— she greatly irritated Thomas.

And now the irritant was turning to him. "Now, Tommy—"

"Doctor Momaday, I—"

"Ah-ah-ah! We agreed not to use titles for these sessions. I asked that we all use our childhood names."

"I cannot call you Little Running Water," Thomas declared.

"Why not?"

"Because if I did, I would only think of an increase in my utility bill."

"Call me Mary then, Tommy."

"Yes, thank you. Mary, please don't call me Tommy. I have never used that name."

"Oh, not even as a child?"

"No."

"You mean," Bobby said, "your mommy never called you Tommy?"

"No—Bobby—she did not."

"But, surely, you called her mommy," Muffie, a mommy herself, stated.

"I suppose, *Muffie,* I may have in the early years of childhood. But she certainly did not allow it after that."

Seeing that she would lose on this, Little Running Water said, "All right, Tom—" A slow and deliberate shaking of Thomas's head stopped her. "Uh, Thomas—what hurts you?"

"I assume a poke in the eye with a sharp stick would do it."

"Thomas …" Doctor Momaday trailed off his name in sad disappointment.

But Thomas was unmoved. "Of course, there's always the classic kick in the groin. I think all of us men, at least, can understand that hurt."

"Thomas, the president—"

"You mean Georgie?"

"The president wants us to examine each other's hurts. And each other's anguish."

"Oh, anguish I can address. Here, now, this moment is anguish enough for me."

"Mr. Vice President!"

"Ah! You really know how to get my attention. Look—Mary, Larry, Bobby, Muffie, and Ricky—I do not want to examine my hurts, and I certainly do not want to examine yours. I do not want catharsis. And, as for my sinus passages, antihistamine does a fine job and supports the American Pharmaceutical Industry." Thomas smiled at that; he thought that was pretty clever. Then, checking his watch, he said, "Look, we've been at this for five hours. Can we call it quits for the day? I still have duties and paperwork to attend to, as I'm sure you all do as well."

"Yes, okay, possibly we should," Mary said. "But will you agree to one thing for me?"

"What's that?"

"Tonight, when you are in your bedroom, alone among your paperwork, will you take one moment out and look for *Tommy*." She pointed toward Thomas's head. "He's in there somewhere, you know. Cute, I bet, towheaded maybe. Mischievous, I'll bet, a real little imp. I would like to meet him."

"Oh, and I'm sure he would like to meet you, *Little Running Water.* As I remember, he was quite retro and loved playing *Cowboys and Indians.*"

Thomas left the room as fast as he could, leaving behind an atmosphere thick with insult. The five left behind had, at first, nothing to say. Or they were at a loss for what could be said. Finally, Larry, known back in Virginia as a lover of a good joke, said, "Hey, Mary! How many Thomas P. Powells does it take to screw in a lightbulb?"

Mary, appreciating the attempt to cut through the mood lightly, smiled and answered, "I don't know, Larry, how many Thomas P. Powells does it take to screw in a lightbulb?"

"It's a moot question 'cause he would never do it 'cause he would never want to get caught screwing when the light came on."

As Thomas left the living room, Agent Wolfe was outside the door, on duty.

"Jeff, is my briefcase and everything in my room?"

"Yes, I had the staff take everything there."

"Fine. Then, unless it is an emergency—" Pain coming from his jaw seemed to pour into his ear, stopping Thomas and wincing his face into an unattractive distortion.

"Sir, are you okay?"

"Yes, fine," the vice president said, irritated at some unfathomable fate and wanting this moment to pass. "Unless," he began again, "it is an emergency, do not disturb me or allow anyone else to."

Thomas P. Powell did not feel right again—calm and collected, centered and controlled—until after he had taken a hot shower, put on a pair of crisp pajamas in the pocket of which he found a note from his wife that made him smile, and had slipped between some luxurious and soft, many thread count, white sheets. He loved those sheets.

On the bed was his briefcase, opened, with stacks of documents with color-coded Post-its alerting him to the subject of the information contained within them. He had just finished reading a most welcome and appreciated letter of invitation, and he pulled his microcassette recorder (a bit retro, but he hated the digital kind) out of the briefcase, checked to see that it was rewound, then started to record:

"Sheila, following is the text of a response to the invitation I received from the American Morality Congress. Dear Stanley, I am pleased to accept your kind invitation to give the keynote address at the AMC's Values and Virtues Convention on March twenty-fifth. As you know, I have always taken great interest in your work and your goals—"

Struck by a massive yawn, Thomas had to stop as his mouth uncontrollably stretched surprisingly wide, the accompanying sound he made being remarkably musical. Thomas sat for a second, wrapped up in this surprise, then recovered; he hit RECORD again when he heard something. Hearing something was not in and of itself surprising. As secure as this lodge in Camp David was, it was an old building, and sounds were carried. People outside, people in hallways, and even cheers from the media room, if someone was watching a ballgame, could all filter through, and one just had to ignore them. But this was different. This was something heard as if it was coming from far away, and it seemed to be an echo, maybe, of the surprising yawn Thomas had just made. Except—and this was the most surprising thing—it was a young yawn. That is a yawn from a young person, presumably male and preadolescent.

Strange—none of the Secretaries had brought their families; they had been forbidden to.

It must have been an echo bouncing off these walls, distorted by some atmospheric anomaly in these wooded hills in Catoctin Mountain Park.

Yes, indeed, that must have been it.

Thomas returned to his dictation.

"And if my appearance can bring the proper attention and recognition they deserve, not to mention serve as a heartfelt thank you, however inadequate, for your continuing support regarding my public service, then I will consider it time well spent indeed."

Thomas paused for a moment of self-reflection and self-debate. Then he continued, allowing something a little bitter to come out.

"And, pursuant to that note, I regret to inform you that the…timetable we have been discussing is now, unavoidably, six years instead of our hoped-for two. President Knight has decided to run in the next general election. Your disappointment, I'm sure, is no less than my own—"

Thomas stopped. It was good to get it out and express it quietly while alone, but no—no, it would not be proper to air this in official correspondence. Thomas rewound the tape for a bit, then stopped and hit play.

... *regarding my public service, then I will consider it time well spent indeed.*

Thomas stopped the little machine and then pushed the RECORD button.

"My warmest regards to you and your family. Sincerely, Thomas P. Powell, Vice President of the United States of America." He finished, snapping off the recorder and placing it back into his briefcase.

Sheila, the vice president's assistant, always smiled when she played back his dictated letters. He did not need to dictate his full name and title each time. It wasn't like she would forget it or the protocol of such letters. It was superfluous of him, a waste of time and breath. And yet it was his time and his breath, and he could, Sheila supposed, do with them as he liked.

Thomas picked up another letter to read, one of the handful of letters from citizens that he received each day, which Sheila picked out as representative of an issue she thought he might be interested in. And he was, but the letter was long and a bit convoluted, and he was weary from hearing for five hours that hurt was hurt, and his eyes closed. Soon, his body relaxed into repose and sunk into the covers, his legs spreading to find their comfort, spreading and slowly pushing his briefcase (with the stacks of documents with color-coded Post-its alerting him to the subject of the information contained within them, not to mention his microcassette) off of the bed and onto the floor with a thump, followed by the screech of the tape machine rewinding his high-pitched dictation.

"What? Huh?" Thomas looked around and then down to see his documents in disarray and the briefcase upside down, but not the recorder, which was pitching high from underneath the bed. "Crap!" Thomas said, and he bent down from the bed to look under it, to see the recorder way under, not in easy reach. Still, he tried nevertheless, mocking gravity as he held on in his place in bed and extended his arm as much as he could, his long middle finger advancing in a stretch to— yes!—reach the recorder, to claw at it, to touch, to miss, to touch again with some pressure, flipping it over and closer, to within grasp, which he applied, securing a grip, pulling in triumph the recorder out from under the bed.

Thomas lifted himself to be once again securely in bed and tried to turn the infernal machine off, but he hit the play button instead.

… And—pursuant to that note …

What!? He was sure he had recorded over that.

… that gray-haired old cracker fart Knight doesn't think we're ready to be president …

He had not said that. He was sure he had not said that—he was, even, it was, in fact, what? It was no longer him on the tape. It was some young boy, some infantile kid, some snide, nasty little imp from the sound of it.

… We're more presidential than that cradle-robbing old reprobate will ever be!

With a raspy inhalation of breath and fear pounding from his chest, Thomas threw the microcassette recorder down onto the bed. He jumped out of it to stare at the possessed instrument as if it were a poisonous snake—a rather vile, ugly, slimy, stinky, poisonous snake. Then he ran into the connecting bathroom, to the sink, turned on the cold-water tap, gathered up the flowing water into cupped hands, and doused his face over and over and over. Why? Why do people do this? Does it at all help? They do it in the movies, and the movies are always right.

It did make him feel better. A cool head, that's what it gave him; that's what he needed, a cool head, which was now very wet. He grabbed a towel and covered his head with it. To dry or to hide? Did it matter? When he pulled the towel down from his head, he hardly recognized the face revealed. He shook his head. He very consciously made his face return to its normal and attractive configuration. Having succeeded in doing that, he took a comb and combed his hair, and then all was set right. It was him. It was he. It was Thomas P. Powell. And that was very reassuring indeed.

Then, Thomas P. Powell noticed a slight movement within his right ear. Within his ear? Yes! Little blonde hairs were struggling to get out. But they were but the advance guard. It was a head, a tiny little towhead that was emerging out of his right ear. Then a slim neck, then small shoulders, then a tiny trunk with its tiny arms, which pushed mightily to excavate itself from a very tight situation, grunting and groaning with melodramatic overreach as only some young boy, some infantile kid, some snide, nasty little imp could.

Resting for a moment, taking time for a breath, the creature crawling out of Thomas P. Powell's right ear looked straight into the mirror, thus straight by reflection at Thomas, and said:

"Gee, it'd be nice if I could get some help here!"

3

Thomas ran from the bathroom and its devil mirror but found himself facing the dresser mirror. There was the thing still, the creature relentless in its struggle, the towheaded, human-shaped object nightmarishly emerging from Thomas's ear.

Thomas contemplated screaming. He weighed the pros and cons and deliberated on the upset to the lodge a blood-curdling, fear-ridden, death-facing, most likely high-pitched, possibly even girl-like, scream would be. The Secret Service would rush in, then all the Secretaries, and then Little Running Water, who would probably declare him insane. And that would make him mad. So no, no, he wouldn't scream—except somewhere deep inside.

The tiny creature gave a mighty, if minor, grunt in what looked to be its final effort to dislodge itself. It was not successful.

Spent, nearly breathless, the creature addressed the vice president. "Hey—you there in the crisp pajamas! Your IQ ain't low, you know, I know that for a fact, got it straight from the synapses, so do you think maybe you could figure out how the hell to get me out of here?"

Thomas leaned into the mirror, enlarging his view of the situation and getting closer to the source of the sound.

"What?"

"What? What do you mean what?"

"I didn't quite hear you. One of my ears is plugged up."

"Oh, so it's my fault, is it? Just get me out of here!"

Thomas reached up slowly to the creature and was about to grab him by the head in a good two-finger, pinchy grip.

"Stop! Are you mad? You'll kill me that way!"

"How …"

"Get your Q-tips, handsome."

"My …"

"In the top dresser drawer right there in front of you. In that slick leather case of yours with the grooming instruments of torture."

The creature was right, of course; there was Thomas's travel grooming kit in which he always placed a sandwich bag stocked with Q-tips. Thomas got several out.

"What do I do with them?"

"Just take one, oh high IQ, and hold it out to me. That's right. Now I'm going to grab onto it really tight, and when I say pull, you pull, okay?"

"Okay."

Thomas did as instructed, taking a Q-tip, holding it by one end, and bringing it up close to the creature protruding from his right ear, slowly trying to align it and bring it within grabbing distance.

The creature grabbed, dug his minuscule hands into the cotton tip, and yelled, "Pull!"

Thomas pulled hard, and the creature held tight to the bulbous end of the Q-tip. It was not an easy job, it hurt, and Thomas formed an image in his brain, of his whole brain, popping out if he succeeded, but succeed he must, for who, honestly, who would want a towheaded little homunculus sticking out of his ear?

The POP! was tremendous, although it was only a pop. It was not a bang or a boom, just a pop, but a tremendous one as the creature, which seemed stretched to its limit, was suddenly released from the ear canal, and Thomas's arm flung out with momentum, flinging the creature out at a blurring speed to smack and stick face first against the wall behind the bed. "Ah, that's better," the homunculus muffled, then pushed itself off the wall with his feet (yes, it did have legs and feet in a most normal manner), executing a backflip to land on the bed and begin bouncing.

"*Wheeeeee!!!!!*"

Up and down the creature went, matched by the nodding of Thomas's head as the vice president could not take his eyes off what he could only assume was a hallucination. Up and down it went, growing with each bounce, from something about two inches tall—*Wheeee!!!!!*—to an apparition of three feet, the size of a child—*Wheeee!!!!!*—but with a body proportioned like an adult—*Wheeee!!!!!*

It was, as one can imagine (indeed, one must imagine, as there is no real-life experience one can draw upon), maddening. What could he do? What could he say? Say…? Yes, he had to address the situation. Or would that make the problem real? But it seemed so real in its surreal way. Still, there it was, bouncing on the bed—bouncing, bouncing, bouncing—the springs springing almost musically, accompanied by constant creaks and groans of metal; it was all so, so….

"Cut that out!" Thomas yelled in admonishment. "That is government property!"

The towheaded, impish creature went up to the ceiling in slow motion, stopped, levitate, and look down upon Thomas. "No, it's not. It's a dolphin!"

As the imp began to fall, the bed metamorphosed into a dolphin. The floor around it became an agitated piece of the ocean the dolphin was swimming through, as if on a water treadmill, arching out of the water, diving in, and arching out again. Thomas could smell the sea, seagulls could be heard in the distance, and foam and spray cooled the room as the imp descended to land on the dolphin's arched back when it surfaced. Then, he rode it with great joy. *Wheeee!!!!*

The whole of what reality was left to Thomas became an endless sea, and he descended into it, sinking among a myriad of colorful fish and strange coral formations, ready to panic over the fact that he wasn't panicking, possibly because he could breathe, oddly, cool, fresh air despite being surrounded by water. Off in the distance was the imp on a dolphin, but closing in on him, faster and faster, closer and closer, finally swimming by gleefully and addressing him with impish pride— "Aren't I cute, towheaded, and mischievous?"—quickly swimming away, back off into the distance.

"Wait!" Thomas yelled, a giant air bubble bursting out of his mouth, growing and growing until it burst and the ocean disappeared.

The sensation of falling into a white void was smacking him, slapping him silly, making his toes curl, his hair scream and his fingernails cry in terror, stopping only when a black, smooth, and slick landscape, like a country of reflective obsidian, was suddenly more than supportive as he thumped onto it, causing a deep, dense, musical note to sound as he bounced up, only to come down again in a series of bounces, each sounding a musical note, the combination of which gave a primitive rendition of "Hail to the Chief." Eventually, the Chief was fully hailed, and Thomas landed for the last time, flat on his back.

"Ooooooo, I bet you that was an absolutely wonderful hurt! A fine hurt!" some infantile kid, some snide, nasty little imp, said in a voice that seemed to come from every direction possible in this impossible landscape.

4

Thomas sat up and looked around. The landscape—black ground, burning sunset sky—stretched forever and featured only sparse black trees of tortured shapes. And there, in front of him, stood the apparition, the creature, the imp. He was still the size of a child and almost looked like a little boy, but there was something far more knowing about his face that no little boy could ever have projected. And yet, he was cute—no, wiseass—no, angelic—no, a rotten little devil—round and round his face seemed to go. It took Thomas a moment to focus on it. Or did he join it in its mercurial shifting? Thomas tore his eyes away from the imp's face and noticed, to his dismay, that he was dressed in blue jeans and a white tee shirt, upon which was printed, HURT IS HURT.

"Yes, such a fine hurt," the imp said. "Would you like to share it with us? I mean, 'hurt is hurt,' ain't it, Little Running Water?"

Out of nowhere, and yet out of everywhere, an image of literal running water formed right next to the imp, no taller than it, and took the shape of Mary Scott Momaday in a complete Hollywood Indian outfit with the addition of a modern-day military general's cap. She carried as her ceremonial staff a giant scalpel, all shiny and sharp.

"Ug! What kind of hurt, Thomas? This kind of hurt!" The little Indian Mary said as she jumped at Thomas and plunged the ceremonial scalpel deep into his right eye, then quickly pulled it out.

It hurt, it burned, it stung, it even tickled. "Ow!" Thomas yelled as he brought his hands to his eye, which he found to be intact, not bleeding, and wholly functional.

"Oooo! Don't share that hurt with me," the imp said.

"No," the little Indian Mary said, "must share hurt!" She plunged the scalpel into the imp's right eye, which sucked it and her in with a considerable SLURP! As Mary's feet disappeared into the imp's eye, there was a loud and sloppy POP!

"I guess I've got *red eye* now," the imp said, grinning, to Thomas, who seemed almost catatonic and certainly non-responsive as he sat there before the imp. "Get it? Ha-ha-ha! *Red eye—red Indian?* Don't you get it? Hey, could you see your way clear to appreciate your own sense of humor? Get it!? *See* your way… Ah, forget it. Now, what other kind of hurt do we got?" The imp moved forward, walking between Thomas's sprawled-out legs. "We did the sharp stick in the eye bit, so I guess the next is …"

As the imp prepared to give Thomas a swift kick in the groin, Thomas was suddenly aroused, up on his feet, screaming and backing up, backing up until the trunk of a weirdly shaped black tree stopped him. "Stay away from me!"

"Ooo, it walks, it talks!"

"Who—what are you?"

The imp shrugged his little shoulders—it was almost cute. "I don't know. Maybe I'm Tommy."

"Tommy?"

"Yes, Thomas, *Tommy*. Get it? Any other hurt you want to share."

"No! Leave me alone."

Thomas dashed between the weirdly shaped trees, trying not to slip on the slick ground.

"How about this one?" Tommy said as the landscape changed quicker than an instant, and Thomas found himself running on top of the president's breakfast table, his tiny, tiny feet (for he was tiny himself) falling on the dark mahogany of the tabletop.

The slap was severe as he ran into a vase, the table's centerpiece.

Flat on his back and winded, Thomas looked up at the stupendously gigantic blossoms of the mixed flowers that shot out of the enormous vase. They were a heaven of riotous colors that made his ears hurt. Or was it the giant, molasses-moving sounds that pounded throughout his head? Holding his ears, Thomas got up and looked through and above and beyond giant cups and glasses, a salt and pepper shaker set, silver utensils, and a gigantic white porcelain coffee carafe with the Presidential Seal on it. He was stunned to see a Mount Rushmore-size President Knight talking to his gigantic self.

"B-E-S-I-D-E-S—Y-O-U-'-R-E—N-O-T—R-E-A-D-Y—T-O—B-E—P-R-E-S-I-D-E-N-T."

An angry, offended, appalled, pissed-off, insulted, infuriated Tommy ran up next to Thomas, shaking his fist up at the giant Mr. President and spitting out venom. "Why you, you old bore! You ineffectual, weak leader! We'll show you!" Tommy whipped out of the ether a square, black box with a big, shiny red button on top, which he gleefully plunged. "Launch missiles!"

The tops of the salt and pepper shakers popped off, and out came two ICBMs, gaining altitude and speeding toward the Rushmore president. But then, midway, they turned and headed back toward Thomas and Tommy.

"Oops! Wrong missiles! Instead of heat-seeking, they're hurt-seeking! Run!"

They turned and ran and ran and ran, passing porcelain and silver and reservoir glasses of water as the missiles, which Thomas perceived to be laughing (or was that Tommy?), bore down on them until they exploded in a bright orange and yellow flash to the sound of glass shattering and tinkling as shards of surreality fell and fell, to finally re-form themselves back into the obsidian landscape with the weird black trees. Thomas smashed onto the shiny black ground with a gong of a sound and a violent reverberation of his body.

As the vibrations subsided, Thomas looked up into the white sky and saw Tommy slowly floating toward him, while also walking in mid-air, pacing back and forth as if trying to solve a puzzlement. When he finally alighted, the pacing continued on the ground.

"All right, so that's not going to work," Tommy said. "So what other way can we get President Knight to become ex-President Knight and—DUM-TA-DUM!—Thomas P. Powell can become the president of these here United States of America. Because, you know, we got to take away our hurt."

"Stop! Stop!" Thomas screamed.

Tommy stopped and was suddenly just a little boy. Weakly and meekly, he said, "Okay."

Thomas got up off the black ground and started to pace himself. "Wake up, wake up, wake up."

Tommy, the little boy went from cute to cunning and whistled a happy tune while walking around Thomas.

"Wake up, wake up, wake up," Thomas continued.

Coming before Thomas, Tommy suddenly leaped up and hovered before his face, "WAKE UP!!!!"

"What?" Thomas stopped pacing; Tommy continued to hover.

In a slow, measured, easy-to-understand, and quiet voice, Tommy addressed Thomas. "President Knight does not think we are ready to be the president of the United States. President Knight does not think we are good enough to be the president of the United States. We have got to get rid of President Knight."

"No! No!" Thomas said, trying to avoid the implications.

"Now, how are we going to do that, Thomas? How? How?"

Thomas turned and ran and continued to scream, "No! No!"

But Tommy ran beside him, his little legs beating the air as he maintained his eye level with Thomas. "I'VE GOT IT! We'll throw him an early retirement party."

Tommy snapped his fingers in an action unworthy of the word's onomatopoeia as what was sounded was a gong, a resounding, resonant gong, followed by tinkles that trickled into place a world of curving, swerving, striped walls enclosing a room of no floor. Yet, there were banquet tables at rest with chairs floating around them filled with dozens of frozen people and one defrosted Thomas. There was a dais in front of them at which stood President Knight and at which floated Tommy.

"Maybe he'll get the hint now," Tommy said as he pulled a large gold pocket watch ticking loudly out of thin air. "Here!" The little imp said to the president as he presented him with the watch. "Good night, Knight!"

But the president whipped out his far larger gold pocket watch that did not tick but went BOOM-BOOM-BOOM and featured the presidential seal in diamonds.

"Ahhhhh," Tommy was mortally disappointed, "Shitenheimer!"

Thomas was running again; running over black, past trees with drooping branches bearing the fruit of broken dreams. Tommy was straddling his neck in hellish piggyback.

"All right, that won't work," the imp said while holding onto Thomas's ears to steady himself, pulling them up, stretching them to keep a rein on Thomas. "Let's see ... What else can we do?" Tommy pulled Thomas's right ear right up to his mouth and, in a conspiratorial voice, whispered, "Should we consider the 'A' word?"

Thomas was suddenly stopped and clothed in nineteenth-century gentleman's wear with laughter floating up at him from a frozen audience and with the imp beside him, lovely in the flowing dress of a nineteenth-century maiden. But the loudest laugh was coming from above, from the Presidential box, wherein sat President Knight sporting an Abe Lincoln beard.

Thomas tried to shout out a warning to the president, but nothing came out of his mouth, and he turned to the lovely Tommy with his eyes pleading.

"Okay! Okay! Not the 'A' thing. But how about a little heart attack?"

President Knight clutched his chest and fell out of his balcony box.

"What...? What have you done?" Thomas found his voice to say.

"What have *I* done? I'm not a doer. I'm just a dreamer," the homunculus said with layers of meaning.

Thomas wanted to scream but found his jaw locked, TMJ pain shooting, and the world spinning and dizzy, becoming the essence of his being. Then the spinning world slowed and settled back to the black landscape, and he found himself sitting on a chair, back in his pajamas, the imp before him, now in matching pajamas.

"Well, you come up with a better idea, then," Tommy said with miniature miff. "I mean, I'm doing all the work here."

Thomas stood up, his attention suddenly elsewhere.

"And just where do you think you're going?"

There was knocking—a faint but urgent knocking.

"Are you going to leave just as opportunity comes knocking?"

The knocking became louder and more urgent.

"Six years! Do you want to wait six years? Can't you hear it—that's destiny knocking."

The voice of Jeff Wolfe came from far away yet very close, from another world yet well planted in Thomas's ear. Jeff Wolfe said, "Mr. Vice President? It's Jeff. Can I come in, Sir?"

"Oh-oh," Tommy said with some surprise. "Gotta go!"

Tommy quickly picked up square tiles from the black ground, letting in morning light until he and the obsidian world were gone, and Thomas stood in the middle of the bedroom, a reality he once knew as solid.

"Mr. Vice President!" Jeff was nearly shouting but in a very dutiful manner.

Thomas desperately pulled himself out of amazement and took deep breaths, quieting panic and fear. "Uh, Jeff, listen, I was up late working last night. Um, would you give my regrets to the others? I intend to sleep a little bit longer."

"I sorry, Sir," Jeff said from beyond the door. "It's an emergency."

"What? Okay, come in."

Thomas found his robe and put it on as Jeff entered. His face, though professionally trained, could not remain professionally passive. "Mr. Vice President, there's been an accident."

What else could Thomas think as the breath seemed to leave his body? In a near whisper, he asked, "The president?"

"No, Sir, no. It's the First Lady and the twins. It was a car accident. The girls are both in critical condition. And, Sir, the, um, the First Lady is dead. The president wants you back in Washington right now, Sir. We have got to go. Right now!"

5

It had been an accident—pure, simple, random, tragic. It was quickly established that it had not been a terrorist attack, no leftover jihadists or agents of the now-out-of-power Russian oligarchs. Nor had it been a lonely, disturbed, mentally agitated non-entity looking to establish a beachhead on the shores of eternity. It had just been a young woman, twenty-two, engaged to a sailor, driving an SUV, texting her opinion of that night's reality show finale, who did not see the yellow go to red and so continued into cross traffic that included the First Lady bringing home the twins from a school event—a chain reaction of reflexes in several drivers not yet understood ended in much damage.

All this was reported to the vice president on the helicopter flight to the Bethesda Naval Hospital in Maryland.

"Why was I not informed last night?"

"The president didn't want to disturb you," Agent Wolfe said. "We were just put on alert in case it was a terrorist attack or whatever. Then the call came in this morning that he wanted you immediately."

But it wasn't "immediately," was it? As the helicopter sped toward the hospital, Thomas did his best to quell the slight lump of insult he felt.

Once the helicopter landed, it was all a rush. Long-legged Secret Service agents set the pace with quick strides downstairs and down corridors. A fit individual, Thomas kept up with no problem, breathing easily and feeding on the state of urgency.

Thomas was guided to a particular door and ushered in, the door closing behind him.

It was a large, private hospital room. There were two beds, each with a broken little girl. They looked horrible, with bandages and multi-colored bruises. Red, purple, and even green made the bruises seem like attached living creatures, maybe sucking the life out of Lisa and Molly.

There were machines between the two beds and machines at either side, some making little noises and with strange appendages that had seemed to reach out and hook themselves to the girls.

President Knight sat on a couch to the side, his head in his hands. He seemed to Thomas to have been folded—or crumpled. Sitting next to him was Mary Connell, the Secretary of State, holding a piece of paper and a pen. Standing close by was Wallace Humphrey, the Supreme Court's Chief Justice for the past twelve years.

"Mr. Chief Justice," Thomas greeted the man whose presence perplexed him. And he acknowledged the other, "Madam Secretary," whose presence did not.

The Chief Justice nodded in return, and Secretary Connell stood up. "Mr. Vice President," she said with palpable sadness.

The president looked up at Thomas. "Mr. President," Thomas moved toward him, "may I express my—"

"Yes, Thomas, thank you. I know. Mary, would you give him the letter."

Secretary Connell handed Thomas the piece of paper she had been holding. Thomas took it and turned it so he could read it. It was on Presidential letterhead, and the few words on it and what they conveyed were, to Thomas, almost unfathomably weird.

"Mr. President, you're—you're resigning?"

The president nodded. "Effective in less than an hour. At the same time, the Chief Justice here will administer the oath of office to you. Kathryn and Charlie are on their way. You'll use the press room here at the hospital."

"But, but...?"

"Thomas, I have no other choice."

"Choice?"

The president turned to the others. "Would you excuse us?"

"Of course, Mr. President," Secretary Connell said.

"We'll see you in the press room," the Chief Justice said as they left.

The president turned to Thomas and felt pity for his confused and uncomprehending state. "Thomas, half my world is dead. And the other half is right here fighting for their lives."

"But does not the country, your duty, have any place in your world?"

"Not anymore—my duty has been condensed to this room."

"Well—"

"Don't try to talk me out of it. The country is strong, Thomas, it will survive. But my girls are the very essence of fragility itself. And when they wake up—" The president's throat closed, and he had to take a deep breath through his nose and blink away some sudden tears. "When they wake up, they will find themselves motherless. How can I ask them to try to heal and recover health without their father's constant care and attendance?"

How could Thomas answer this man he had so lately mocked as weak yet now seemed a true tower of strength, suddenly crumbling before him?

"You—you said I was not ready to be president."

"Yes, but what I did not tell you is—no one ever is."

6

The huge and ultra-thin video screen had a strange presence in the Oval Office. It was like a rectangular, twenty-first-century gash on the mock-eighteenth-century Georgian north wall, right above and dominating the white marble fireplace. But it was terrific for videoconferences and great for watching movies. And, on occasion, it was used to display a video loop of purple mountain majesties and amber waves of grain, spacious skies, and fruited plains, not to mention shining seas. Often, though, it was the news of the day or coverage of the president that beamed off the thin screen.

At this moment in our story, there was a large image of President Thomas P. Powell accompanied by a graphic stating: THE POWELL PRESIDENCY: THE FIRST 100 DAYS.

We now return to a CBS Special Report, The Powell Presidency, the First One Hundred Days.

On the widescreen, two men sat facing each other in the Oval Office: President Powell and the current anchor of the CBS Evening News, a going-grey man of serious demeanor. In the actual Oval Office, five men watched, also with serious demeanors.

Mr. President, we only have a few moments left, so, to conclude, I now would like to turn to what has become infamously known as the Great Weekend Massacre, which occurred about one month into your presidency.

The president on the screen smiled, and the president watching did not.

I must disagree with that characterization, which the media have perpetuated. The changes in my cabinet were simply a matter of course.

The newsman was good at masking his feelings, but slight incredulity did skim his visage.

But surely you can see how the wholesale dumping of President Knight's cabinet over a weekend struck many people as, well, as abrupt, if not callous.

The president answered without hesitation.

I had made my decision. Should I have made changes piecemeal? Slowly causing untold anxiety among several people? That would hardly have been fair. I felt that if we were going to make a change, we should make it quickly so that everyone could get on with their lives. And, I think you will agree that the new cabinet members, once confirmed, stepped in and grabbed the reins of their responsibilities quickly, and the government business was not held up by even one day.

The anchor shifted slightly in his seat as he shifted some papers.

Some have said that the burden you placed on the Senate to confirm so many high-level officials simultaneously diluted its power, causing them to do only a cursory job in their considerations and deliberations.

The president of the screen smiled again, and the president in the room could not help smiling as well.

Well, as you know, the president does not control the Senate. It could have taken as much time as it felt it needed. But my good friends in the Senate knew the need for a smooth transition. My staff and I worked tirelessly to make sure that my nominees—in every case—deserved confirmation.

And with that, the anchor knew he had gotten the president's final word.

Well, we are out of time. Thank you, Mr. President.

"Great! Great interview!" Eric Burton, the White House Press Secretary, said as he switched off the video screen with a remote and stood up, almost as if to take a bow for an excellent job well done. The other men in the room took no notice of him, which was appropriate as he was but a conduit to the press, but it was no less an abrasion on his ego as Burton was, despite appearances and manner, a human being born of woman.

"It went well," said John Sayers, the president's chief of staff. *Don't you think?*

"I think your message regarding the Russian debt," Secretary of State Herman Berger addressed the president, "came across unambiguously clear."

"Do you think President Kostroma," Thomas addressed the room and posterity, "was listening to it at Blair House?"

"We're sure of it," Berger said. He should now be well aware that he won't be able to play the emotion card at the summit tomorrow."

"He's quite an emotional man himself, I understand," Thomas said, presenting it as a potential weakness to be aware of, deal with, and exploit.

"We have files on his emotions at the State Department, Mr. President," Berger reported on the facts—and his competence. "But that does not mean he is not cold and calculating when he wants to be."

"Yes, that certainly is true. Thank you, Herman, for joining us. I know how busy you have been preparing for this week."

"I've put in place an excellent staff, Sir. But I should be getting back to it."

"Of course. I will see you in the morning."

As the Secretary of State left the Oval Office, Thomas turned to his chief-of-staff. "John, do you have an assessment on the domestic?"

"What's to assess? Happy times, happy prosperity, happy news. No one ever killed the messenger of that."

"The latest economic figures are off. As has just been pointed out in this interview."

"A mere blip, Sir—a mere blip. As *you* pointed out."

"Let us hope."

Thomas then turned to the other man in the room. He was a man almost tall, almost handsome, almost bald. He had grey eyes that seemed mild but were penetrating, nevertheless. He had a strange mouth with a full lower lip yet a thin upper lip. But the upper lip was canopied by a mustache fuller than his lower lip. He was only five years older than Thomas. Still, he seemed older not just because of Thomas's youthful looks, which had not yet faded, but because he had placed himself in that position from the moment that he sought out Thomas, fresh from his moment of heroism, to tutor him on maintaining his quick celebrity status and turning it into opportunity, into a platform, into a voice. It was Stanley James, whose American Morality Congress had mobilized the vote for the current second-term Governor of California, and who had convinced that governor that appointing Thomas to a vacated-by-death congressional seat would be political gold. It was Stanley James whom Thomas felt closest to because Stanley had always seemed to understand Thomas's mind best, possibly because he had often shaped it.

"Stanley, do you think your people at the AMC appreciated the comments?"

"I'm sure they are as ecstatic as I am, Mr. President. To finally have a president in the White House who is not only a man of high moral fiber and principles, but one willing to advocate a nationwide return to values and virtues—"

One of several phones on the president's desk rang. It was a gently melodic ring.

"Excuse me," the president said. The three men started to leave. "No, please, stay. It will only be Kathryn." He picked up the phone and eagerly said, "Hi! Did you see it?"

Kathryn was away in California, in a large hotel suite, sitting on the side of a large bed. Her son was sitting next to her, hugging a giant, stuffed Mickey Mouse.

"Yes, it went very well, didn't it?"

"That seems to be the consensus here."

"Do you think you may have come down a little hard on the dependent children issue?"

"No, I just reiterated the actual issue: Dependent on whom? Fits in nicely with my personal responsibility campaign." Thomas turned to address James. "Don't you think, Stanley?"

"I do, Mr. President."

"Oh," Kathryn almost whispered into the phone, "Stanley's there."

"He just happened to be in town."

"Oh, I'll bet. Speaking of dependent children, do you have a moment to say hi to Charlie?"

"Charles? What is Charles doing awake?

"He wanted to see his daddy on TV."

"Well, Kathryn, we would have had the video. You know this trip has got to be tiring for him, he should be getting his—"

"Daddy! I saw you on TV!"

"Excellent, Charles. Did you like it?"

"Yes, you were very handsome!"

"Thank you, Charles. Now you need to go to bed."

"I've got a neat bed. It's bouncy. I've jumped all over it."

"Well, now, Charles, remember, that's government—" Thomas stopped himself. What? Why? He was wrong, but had he…? "I mean *hotel* property. So, you will be careful."

"Okay. Night! I love you, Daddy!"

"Very good, Charles. I will see you when you get home."

"I'm back." It was Kathryn.

"Okay. Has it been a good trip?"

"Very nice. Mrs. Kostroma and the kids loved the whole Disney experience. By the way, I also got a call today locking down the program for the Literacy Conference and—"

"Uh, can't talk about that right now."

"Well, okay. But as soon as I get back."

"Well, yes, of course. Once we put this summit behind us."

"Thomas…?"

"I really must go. Give Charles a kiss for me, bye."

Thomas put down the phone and gave a moment's thought to a pending issue, then turned to Stanley James.

"Stanley, real quick, as John can tell you, we hope by the end of the week to be able to confirm that I can still speak at the Values and Virtues Convention, but a conflict has come up—"

"Mr. President," Stanley James's grey eyes darkened just a little, "we pushed back the convention to give you some more settling-in time."

"Yes, I appreciated that. But President Knight had committed to speak to the Literacy Conference, and it's turning out that it and your function are on the same night. Now, as you know, the literacy effort is being overseen by the First Lady, so we are just trying to juggle a few things."

"Well," James pursed his lips in a manner many who knew him were familiar with, "Thomas, I'm sure you'll do the, um—the right thing."

"I always try, Stanley."

The door to the Oval Office opened, and the president's secretary, Sheila, announced, "Mr. President, Dr. Meier is here."

"Fine," Thomas said. "Send him in."

As Dr. Meier, physician to the president, entered, Thomas held out his hand to Stanley. "Thank you for joining us this evening, Stanley." It was both a sincere sentiment and a necessary dismissal.

"It was an honor to be asked, Mr. President."

As Stanley James left, Dr. Meier, a Navy lieutenant commander, entered.

"Doctor, one moment, please," Thomas said as he signaled his press secretary over.

"Eric, you did a good job negotiating with the network."

"Thank you, Sir. Wanted to make sure that question about the cabinet came up last."

"Yes, that was excellent thinking. But one thing—did you have a problem with my tie?"

"No, Sir, I picked it out. I rather liked it."

"The knot was askew, Eric."

"Sir?"

"When the sound man put on my lapel mic, he pulled on my tie and displaced the knot. I could have no way of knowing this, of course. But the upshot was, tonight, the president of the United States looked like a damn local yokel to millions of Americans."

"Oh, no, Sir, I don't believe—"

"Take me seriously on this, Eric. From now on, for every television appearance, you will make a last check of the position of my tie. If it is not perfect, you will stop the proceedings; you will dead-stop them until you make it perfect. Understood?"

"Yes, Sir, I understand. I'm sorry. It won't happen again."

"I know it won't, Eric, good night."

Eric Burton failed to acknowledge Dr. Meier as he left.

"Doctor, I'm sorry to have to schedule you in so late," The president said as he gestured for the doctor to sit.

"Mr. President, I have not had a normal schedule since I entered medical school. I wouldn't know what to do if I did have one." The doctor sat, placing a small laptop computer on the table before him. He opened it and called up the president's file.

"Yes, those who serve. Our life is not our own. So—my health?"

"There have been no perceivable changes from the last physical I conducted when you took office. You are both a non-smoker and a non-drinker, so you have no problems related to those activities. Your blood pressure is perfect.

Thomas was delighted to hear it. He had always felt that good health was a moral imperative. "Pretty good for the leader of the Free World, then?"

"Sir, despite what the layman thinks, high blood pressure does not always indicate stress in your life. Your TMJ was far more indicative. Is that still giving you any problems?"

"No—no, it is not. I have not even thought about it in months. I guess I am sleeping the sleep of the innocent now."

Dr. Meier typed a note. "Mmm, one other thing, which I forgot to ask about during the physical—any reoccurrence of that nightmare?"

"Nightmare?"

"You mentioned during that first physical. You had it on the night before you became president." The doctor read from the computer screen. "'A surreal, frightening nightmare, unlike anything I have ever had before.' That's what you said at the time."

"Something else I have completely forgotten about. But then, this job is somewhat all-consuming."

The doctor typed another note and then closed the laptop. "Well, let me know if there is any reoccurrence. Mind, body—so close."

7

The Executive Mansion never seemed empty and abandoned. Even on days with no evening events—a State dinner or a performance at the White House—there were always, at least, Marines on guard in their impressively neat uniforms, late-working policy implementers wandering corridors sincerely wondering how they would implement a particular policy—and amorous interns, loving the atmosphere of executive power after hours.

Not sexually amorous, as gossip and some confirmed accounts might suggest interns naturally are, but history, policy, duty, fame, and power amorous, none of which is necessarily bad.

Sarah Newitz was one of those amorous interns. She saw the world as enormous, complex, challenging, and needing order. Those who strived to bring order fascinated her. She hoped one day to fascinate others. Until then, she would support and aid with alacrity. And take extreme pleasure in passing by the main "actors" of the day in the extraordinary story of America, the grand epic of the world. Such as the president of the United States, who was passing her while walking alone, heading for the elevator to his residence, who had passed her before, often, and had never once failed to nod and acknowledge.

After leaving the Oval Office, Thomas walked alone down a White House corridor. He took a sober delight in those who passed him, saying, "Good night, Mr. President." It also allowed him to respond sincerely with wishes for their own good nights. Marines, policy wonks, interns, he saw them all not as cogs in a great machine but as spokes in the spinning wheel he was the hub of. He was determined to always, very consciously, appreciate them, especially given that serving him would probably be the highlight of their lives.

There was a large, ornate mirror along the corridor where Thomas had the habit—built up since his days as vice president—of stopping to check the current condition of his tie. Straight? Cinched? Sincere? Even in moments like this, when the tie would soon be taken off and hung neatly in his closet. But then, it was not the tie the president was checking but his confidence. The meter for which resided somewhere in his eyes and the—

A stake of frozen fear impelled his chest with a whoosh, and something tight held his breath captive in a small, dark place.

The homunculus, the imp, the tiny Tommy in like suit, in like tie—straight, cinched, and sincere—with his hair combed as Thomas combed his, smiling a not pleasant smile, eyes dark with a secret plan, was emerging without effort from Thomas's right ear.

"Excuse me, Mr. President, are you okay?" Sarah Newitz had silently been reveling in her closeness to fame and power when she had seen the president's eyes widen and heard his breath call out for help.

"What?" Thomas turned to the intern, who had come up to stand by his side. She wanted to give him a comforting touch but dared not to, daring only to grace him with concerned eyes.

"I'm sorry—I heard—uh …"

Thomas turned back to the mirror. The horrible homunculus was nowhere to be seen. Did he go back in? Was he out about somewhere? Relieved of the image—even if he feared it might be short-term—Thomas turned around to the intern. "Oh, yes, no, I'm fine. I just—I just suddenly remembered that I wanted to get a little boy or something for Charles, uh, for tomorrow, uh, when he comes back."

"You mean, like a playmate?"

"Playmate? What are you talking about?"

"I'm sorry, Sir. I thought you said you wanted to get Charlie a little boy…?"

"Boy? No—*toy*, I want to get him a toy. But I guess it's too late now."

With great eagerness to fulfill a presidential request, Sarah, the intern, said, "Oh, I could do that for you, Sir!"

"You could?"

"Of course. A stuffed animal or something?"

"Uh, yes, sure, that would be fine."

"I'll take care of it on my way in tomorrow, Sir."

"Okay, Goodnight."

"Goodnight, Sir."

Thomas entered the elevator that went up to the family residence and allowed himself—once the doors came together, closing him in—a big shudder and a bit of hyperventilation.

Going up!

It was the sound of the imp's voice, here and now, a screech, a gong, a siren, and a scream all in one head-piercing, concentrated puncture of Thomas's eardrums.

The UP button lit.

The car ascended with unusual speed.

Thomas collapsed to the floor.

The car stopped with unusual abruptness.

Thomas shot up and slammed against the ceiling of the elevator. Then he floated down, light as a feather, with the lilt of the Blue Danube Waltz in his ears, to land on his feet just as the elevator doors opened. He rushed out into the central hall and the West Sitting Room, slamming the door behind him. He positioned himself right in the center of the room—as if, in the center, he would find peace—and tried his very best to plant his feet.

"It was the doctor," Thomas presidentially addressed himself. "He reminded me of that nightmare, that's it. Planting it in my brain, which is tired and which projected the, uh, the sub-conscious, uh—"

The president's head exploded in red, white, and blue flames.

Or seemed to as a rocket-shaped Tommy was launched from the president's skull and flew in crazy loops all about the room, red-spewing flames, blue-bursting sparkles, and white, puffy smoke coming out of its tail as a high-pitched whistling of "Hooray for the Red, White, and Blue" pierced the air.

Thomas threw his hands up to his ears and hunched over, possibly in pain, possibly in fear, perhaps to escape.

Then, a fleshy, warm weight landed on his shoulders, which seized the president's neck with a grip of his little legs and the president's head with a hug from impish arms.

"Horsey! Horsey! Let's play horsey!" The gleeful weirdness yelled and whooped.

"What the hell?"

Thomas started buckling like a bronco, trying to shake the putrid weight off his shoulders.

"Yahoo! Ride'em cowboy!"

"GET OFF ME!"

Thomas reached up and grabbed the terror and flung it up and away.

The little living presidential doll went up—then came down with a bounce—then back up—then down—then up—then down once more. "Bouncy! Bouncy! Bouncy!" The imp laughed like a maniac; Thomas fell into an easy chair. Then, the imp slowly floated downward while smoothing his suit and straightening his tie.

Once landed, the imp stood solidly on the ground, directly in front of Thomas, and was perfectly calm. Smiling, he addressed Thomas with the causal question, "Did you miss me?"

Thomas did not answer. He looked around the room with a quizzical face, refusing to see the tiny, distorted mirror image of himself. "Isn't that funny?" he asked the universe as calmly as he could. "I don't remember going to bed. I am in the middle of that nightmare again—obviously, that is clear, no doubt about it—and yet, I don't remember going to bed."

"That's because you didn't go to bed, big boy," the imp said, walking up to Thomas. "And I'm no nightmare. Although that said, I'm no dream either."

The imp looked around the room, satisfied with what he saw. "Well, we did it! Pres-i-dent of these here United States of America! I'd be impressed, but I know recent history."

"We—*we* did it?"

"Well, not in so many car crashes. But you got your destiny, didn't you?"

"This is crazy. This is *not* real."

"Oh, thanks. I love having my existence questioned. You want me, at my tender years, to have a problem with self-esteem, with existential angst, with no basic, loving confirmation of who I am?"

"Uh ..."

"Well? Do you?

"Well—"

"Here, look, touch me."

Thomas reached out, then hesitated.

"Go ahead, touch me."

Taking a breath, Thomas reached out to the imp's head—and put his hand right through it. It was frightening. And yet full of wonder.

"Are…are you a ghost?" He asked as he pulled his hand out of the imp's head.

"Who knows? I just thought it would freak you out. Try again."

Again, Thomas reached out as the imp turned to marble—Makrana marble, from India, just like the marble used in the construction of the White House. Thomas touched the cold stone and then rapped on it.

"Solid, huh?" The marble-headed imp said.

Thomas pulled his hand back and looked at it as if it also might change.

"One more time! This is fun!"

Thomas, as if possessed, as if addicted, reached out for the imp's head again, landing on a soft sponge. He gathered the imp's head in his fist, squeezed, compressed, and reduced it to a tiny, scrunched-up ball. Then he let it go, and the imp's head slowly expanded back to normal.

"He-he-he-he-he! Talk about messing with someone's head! Get it? Messing with someone's head! Ha-ha-ha!"

Thomas no longer felt anything. Not panic, not confusion, not fear; not cold, not hot, not happy, not sad. He wanted to float away from himself, to position himself in some seat of truth. "Subjectively sensing my mental condition," he said to himself as he was desperate to hold onto the self that was, he hoped, him, "I am obviously ill. But am I incompetent? If so, duty requires that I hand over the reins of power to the next in line of succession. And as the stupid Senate has not yet confirmed my new vice president, that means the Speaker of the House. Unfortunately, the speaker is from the other party and is a woman I despise. Therefore, I can only try, in my current insanity, to retain at least a vestige of sanity so that I can competently handle the affairs of state."

The imp watched this, fascinated and appalled. "Do you talk to yourself often?"

The intrusion was an unfortunate imposition of a very unusual reality. Thomas had no choice; he would have to deal with it.

"Who or, or what are you?"

"Me? I'm Tommy! And I'm exhausted. And I need to get out of these clothes."

Tommy turned and marched out of the West Sitting Hall and into the master bedroom. Thomas watched him for a second, then followed. When he entered his bedroom, he found Tommy in a miniature version of his favorite pajamas, pulling the covers back. Then he climbed into the big bed like a little boy would. Once settled and comfy, he said, "It's going to be great to get a good night's sleep. I need my rest so that, you know, we can get started tomorrow. G'night!" Tommy dropped his head on the pillow and fell asleep, snoring cute, short, musical snores.

Thomas did not know what to do. He was not going to crawl into bed with this homunculus version of himself, that's for sure. That would have been just too strange. He walked over to a desk, sat down, took off his tie, neatly laid it down, and then took up a thick, bound document waiting for his review. The cover was embossed: RUSSIA, A CURRENT ASSESSMENT: A SPECIAL REPORT FOR THE PRESIDENT OF THE UNITED STATES BY THE AMERICAN MORALITY CONGRESS.

Thomas turned around to see Tommy sleeping angelically in bed. Then, he turned back to the report to escape the horror of the homunculus by reading the wisdom of the AMC.

8

Thomas had an uncomfortable yet blessedly dreamless sleep that night. Uncomfortable because he had spent it slumped over the desk, his head resting on the AMC's account of all the rampant immorality that had returned to Russia after the strong influence of national pride had left when the central, putrid oligarch-controlling throwback to the Soviet era had been surprisingly voted out of office. Dreamless because after the bedtime nightmare, what was there to dream about?

Vague consciousness sparked, his eyes opened, and light sliced in. In a now-crumpled suit, Thomas arose to stiffness and pain in muscles and joints. He stood, stretched, and wiped a tiny bit of drool off page sixty-four of the report from the American Morality Congress. He looked at the clock and saw it was late for him; he never slept this late. His self-discipline was such that he awoke every morning at the same time to the minute. He did not need an alarm clock, his wife, or a White House staff member to wake him. To oversleep was strange, surreal, and as weird as the little homunculus—

Thomas looked at his bed. It was perfectly made to military standards. No one had slept in it the night before. No one was in it now.

There was no time to consider this, this—fact? But a shave, a shower, physical and mental revival, and fresh clothing—these were facts he could handle. He quickly set about to do so.

Downstairs, in the hallway before the elevator, John Sayers, the president's chief-of-staff; Eric Burton, the presidential press secretary;

and Secretary of State Herman Berger stood waiting with some concern for the President.

Sayers checked his watch, not for the first time in the last minute or two. "I have never known this man to be late."

"Calm down. He's on his way," Berger said.

"Perhaps we should send up one of the Secret Service agents to —"

The arrival of the elevator car from the residence cut Burton off, and all three men were relieved when the doors opened, and the president walked out. He went directly up to his press secretary. "Eric, how is this?"

Burton knew immediately what the president was referring to, as the knot of his tie was askew. "Uh, may I?" Burton indicated the knot and his desire to right it.

"Yes, yes, of course," Thomas said with impatience.

Burton undid the president's tie and started to re-tie it, somewhat hampered by the flow of the president's attention.

"John," the president addressed Sayers.

"Yes, Sir?"

"I want you to get ahold of the National Weather Service."

"The National Weather Service, Sir?"

"Yes, I want to find out if there were any strange atmospheric disturbances or anomalies last night, especially here."

"Here? You mean the DC area?"

"No, here! Right here, the White House. Right above us!"

"That localized?"

"Yes!"

As Thomas spoke all his words with agitated movements, Burton found it challenging to get the knot just right. "Sir? Excuse me…?"

"What!?"

"Well, Sir, if you could hold still for just a minute."

"Oh, yes, sorry."

Thomas took in a large breath, let it out, and froze.

Sayers's face seemed frozen as well, into a quizzical visage. "And I'm to ask about atmospheric anomalies?"

"Yes," the president said, stiff-necked, "anything strange in the atmosphere. Also, same question for the night before I took office."

Done, Burton pulled himself back to look at his work. "Okay, Sir. Looks fine."

"Fine, let's go. And John, the night before I became president, check for conditions over Camp David that night, okay?"

The president took the lead, and the men started down the corridor, passing the art and antiques on display that kept the White House somewhere in the middle of the nineteenth century. But that was how the Powells liked it, so that was how it was. Thomas particularly liked the Gilbert Stuart, full-length portrait of George Washington, new president, out of uniform, standing by a small table, gesturing towards…?

Towards a big bottle of pills?

Thomas stopped suddenly before the painting. Pills? He looked up at George, the indispensable man, and saw Tommy, the inconceivable imp.

"Hey-ye, hey-ye, hey-ye," the well-suited, well-painted homunculus under George's white wig barked, "Do you suffer from active denial? If so, try George Washington's *I Cannot Tell a Lie* pills. Simple, fast, and effective, they will have you telling the truth in no time—even to yourself!"

"Sir," John Sayers noticed a shift in the president's face, an expansion of his eyes, and a jerk, almost of his head. "Are you all right?"

Thomas put his hand up to his right jaw. "Damn! I'm afraid my TMJ has returned."

"Oh, I'm sorry, Sir. Should I call for the doctor?"

"No," Thomas said, turning his full attention to Sayers, "it must run its course. But—but you should know, John, that when it hits me, it is severe. Takes me out of myself for a moment. I will try not to show it, but…."

"I will cover for you, Mr. President. Don't worry."

"Good, now—" Thomas sought out the nearest Secret Service agent and approached him. "Agent, where's Jeff Wolfe?"

"Just going off duty, Sir. He had the night shift."

"Get him."

"What?"

"Now! Now! Call him on your radio thingy and get him here now!"

"Yes, Sir!"

As the agent started talking into his radio, Sarah Newitz, the intern Thomas had spoken to the night before, shyly approached the men. "Hello, hi! Excuse me, Mr. President?" Sarah held up an adorably cute (by her estimation) stuffed animal raccoon. It was two-tone in color—bright pink and deep purple—and the group looked at both her and it with some confusion, a slight annoyance, and not a small amount of fear that she would make it talk in a high-pitched, cutesy voice.

"Yes?" said Thomas. "What is it?"

"Here it is, Sir." She stepped forward to hand it to the president, but the agent intercepted her and took the raccoon from her hands with very little common courtesy, frightening Sarah, who found the agent tall, square, and machine-like. "It's, um, it's just the toy, Sir. Last night, you said you had forgotten to get Charlie a welcome home toy, so I said I would and—"

"Yes, yes, I remember now. It's okay, Agent." Thomas took the raccoon from the agent and gave it a good look, then smiled and looked at Sarah. "Yes, this will be fine. Is it from a cartoon or something?"

"No, I don't think it's famous or anything. But, you know, it's really huggable."

"Huggable?"

"Kids like huggable. Even boys. I mean, you know, young ones like Charlie."

"Well, I am sure he will love it, and I thank you very much. Can you give the receipt to my secretary? I will have her reimburse you from my personal account."

"Oh, that's not necessary, Sir, I'm happy—"

"Rules, uh…?"

"Sarah."

"Sarah. There are rules to follow. Always follow the rules, Sarah."

Fast-paced steps were heard coming down the hallway. It was Jeff Wolfe. "You wanted me, Mr. President?" Jeff asked while still some feet away.

"Yes, uh, excuse me, everyone," the president said, leaving to meet Jeff and pulling him down the corridor, away from the others.

"Sir, we are running late," Herman Berger said after them.

"Won't be a minute, Herman," Thomas announced, then turned to Jeff. "Jeff, get onto the CIA, the FBI, the FCC, and any other agency you think appropriate. Ask them if anyone by any chance monitored any strange radio transmissions or, I don't know, microwaves, I guess, or infrared. The whole spectrum; tell them to cover the whole spectrum."

"I'm sorry, Sir, I don't understand."

"Waves! Waves, Jeff! Find out if any strange waves are hitting the White House. And Camp David! Camp David on the night of—the night before I became president. Remember, we were there."

"I remember, Sir. I'm just not sure they can be that specific."

"Jeff, I have seen pictures of the King of England picking his nose! Surely, they can tell me this. So, find out. But—but report only to me."

"Sir," John Sayers walked over to the president and Jeff. "President Kostroma is waiting."

"Oh, yes, of course," Thomas said while giving Jeff a look of scared understanding. Then he turned to the group of men, took a deep breath, looked around at all the paintings on the hallway walls, and let out a relieved breath when he saw nothing but ordinary reality. He stood himself a little taller, becoming as presidential as possible. He suddenly smiled, said to the men, "Let's go," and led them to the Diplomatic Reception Room.

Russian President Kostroma was in the ground floor Diplomatic Reception Room with his contingent of advisors, just wondering what the delay was, when the president of the United States, smiling broadly, entered with his contingent and walked directly over to Russia's young but seasoned, democrat, a new face on the world stage, but one the media was loving.

"President Kostroma," Thomas said in greeting, holding out his right hand, which President Kostroma found to be holding a pink and purple stuffed animal. Kostroma was unsure if it was a typical American diplomatic gift or a strange American joke. Kostoma's lack of surety found a home on his face, and Thomas saw that clearly and then realized what he was offering. "Oh, sorry," Thomas passed the raccoon from his right to his left hand, "a gift for my son."

President Kostroma took Thomas' now-empty right hand and shook it, "President Powell. That is, I think, a raccoon."

"Yes, I guess it is."

"A native of North America, I believe."

"Uh, yes, that is right."

"But introduced into my country for their fur."

"Really? I did not know that."

"Russia is a cold country. Fur is valued."

"Yes, I can understand that."

"Nevertheless, the animal is a damn nuisance to some."

"Oh?"

"But one as—strangely attractive as that one could be a nuisance to no one. I'm sure your son will love it."

The two presidents and their contingents moved outside to the White House lawn and walked to a waiting area before the helicopter pad, where Marine One, carrying their spouses and their children, was landing. President Kostroma smiled broadly when he saw his wife's face in one of the helicopter's windows and waved enthusiastically. President Powell stood at attention with his arms behind his back, effectively hiding the pink and purple raccoon. Whether he was hiding it from Charlie, keeping it a surprise, or hiding it from the media-filtered world, keeping it from being an embarrassment, was known only to himself.

Marine One's doors opened. Mrs. Kostroma and her children, a boy of four and a girl of seven, emerged, followed by the First Lady and Charlie. Kathryn held onto Charlie's hand, and Charlie held onto his stuffed Mickey Mouse, but the Kostroma kids were allowed to run free, and they did so, excitedly running across the lawn to their father, who squatted to receive them, taking the blow of their affection and absorbing it in an enormous, encompassing hug. Then he stood, scooping up his son and swinging him around once, then twice, then a thrilling third time, while his daughter jumped up and down demanding the same.

Knowing fun, when he saw it, Charlie broke from his mother's grip and ran to his father, yelling, "Swing me, Daddy! Swing me!" all the way there and continued the chant while jumping in place before his father. The president bent towards the young boy, placing a hand on the child's shoulder, tampering him down from his joyful high, "Not now, Charles, later maybe." Although the boy had no words for it and could hardly understand it, he felt the sharp pain of disappointment and possible future irritation. But then his father brought forth—"Uh, here,"—the fuzzy explosion of pink and purple. Two eyes went big, one little mouth flew open wide with delight, and one corporate mascot dropped unceremoniously to the ground. Charlie, all pain now gone, the future now a bright pink and purple, grabbed the raccoon and hugged it tightly.

Kathryn, surprised her husband came bearing a gift, said, "Nice raccoon."

"Uh—it is a native of North America," the president said as if that gave that which was personal a professional excuse.

"Really?" The First Lady said as she picked up Mickey. "But it's not like I didn't buy him two dozen toys in California."

"But I love this one best!" Charlie said. And he did, he certainly did, for it was not the cuteness, the huggability, the vibrant color scheme that engendered such tender thrill, but—indeed—the thought—and who thought it—that counted.

The two presidential families, and all the others, headed to the White House along the red carpet. President Kostroma, a big man, carried both his children, an image and concept that Charlie found quite appealing.

"Carry me, Daddy! Carry me!" the boy said, jumping with his raccoon up into Thomas's arms, into a one-arm, tight hug around his father's neck as his other arm hugged and held the raccoon. Without intention, Charlie awkwardly pushed the plush animal into the president's face. Thomas grabbed his son, secured him, and reared back his head to see the raccoon's face suddenly become that of the imp.

"Cute, ain't I?" Tommy the raccoon said with a crookedly cute smile and crazy eyes.

Having no means of fight, Thomas' instincts moved him to flight. But to where? And how? He swung to the right to escape, but the pink and purple imp just rode along. Still, to turn to the right again and again and again was all Thomas could think to do—although thought had little to do with it.

"*Wheeeee!*" A delighted Charlie yelled out as he went on a whirligig ride. "More! More!"

Thomas stopped. "What?"

"Again, Daddy!"

Americans, Russians, men, women, Marines standing at attention, and the media standing in bemusement. They were all watching, and by watching, they obliged the president of the United States to continue. And so, he did so, giving his son a fast-spinning ride.

"*Wheeeee!!!!!!!!*" the delighted Charlie exclaimed and laughed.

Thomas entered the Diplomatic Reception Room dizzy.

"That was fun, Daddy!" Charlie said, still hanging on.

The large party surrounding the presidents and their families was mainly all smiles. The few exceptions felt some—or someone's—embarrassment.

"Yes, well, you better go to your mother now," Thomas said as he handed Charlie to Kathryn. Glancing at the pink and purple critter, he saw it was back to normal now—again, just the image of a fanciful raccoon, a North American native.

The president's chief-of-staff walked up to him, "Are you okay, Mr. President?

Thomas started to straighten himself, his suit, his tie. Eric Burton came up to help.

"Yes, yes, of course," the president said. "I was—I was just having fun with Charles. Is that okay with you, John?"

"Mr. Sayers," President Kostroma said as he walked up, "are you not a father? It can make one joyously dizzy! Right, President Powell?"

"Yes," Thomas remembered to smile, "dizzy would be the word for it."

The Oval Office was the most famous room in America, possibly the world. Its depiction in numerous filmed dramas and its documentation in countless photos made it as familiar to most people as their living rooms, as comfortable and oddly cozy as their bedrooms: Democracy in action. But for Thomas, it was a sacred space that brought into the material world all the profound and prideful feelings that he felt had flowed smoothly throughout his being from the day he had become the president. It was not so much that he felt most like a president in the room, but that the room was the presidency itself, and one could not help but want to honor that and never sully it.

The two presidents from two countries, often at odds, sat facing each other. Neither face revealed thoughts or emotions. They sat in chairs before the fireplace as their contingents sat on the two couches extending out from those chairs. Despite the White House having the finest climate control technology, the atmosphere was thick and heavy as President Kostroma broke an uncomfortable silence.

"President Powell, my predecessor took Russia to the brink of another dictatorship, making our constitution and democracy a sham. I have managed to reverse some of his damage, but—"

"Which is why America counts you as a good friend," Thomas cut him off, knowing instinctively that a plea would be reiterated; his declaration of so much more to do would be his begging line.

"A 'good friend' would be more understanding in the matter of this debt," Kostroma said dryly with no prideless plea in his voice.

"A good friend would encourage you to practice the virtue of fulfilling your obligations. We value virtues here in America. For example, we were obligated to destroy terrorism, and we fulfilled that obligation."

"Really? I always thought it had more to do with the discovery of how to efficiently split hydrogen from oxygen, giving the world a cheap, renewable energy source." The Russian Federation president was an intelligent, aware man, a former professor of history who had never forgotten a lesson. "Without the petrodollars behind them, did not the terrorists just mainly dry up and die? Not to mention what it did to *my* country's main source of wealth."

Thomas managed to ignore the pointed implications. "It was America who made that discovery."

"Was it? My apologies for my shaky history. I was under the impression that it was an Indian scientist working in London."

"Yes, but funded by America."

"With money borrowed from China."

"A debt we have paid back."

"And was not the engineer who figured out how to convert pre-existing autos to hydrogen a brilliant woman from Japan?"

"The West, then. Led by America."

"Japan? The West?"

"Japan has been a part of the West from the day we bombed Hiroshima."

President Kostroma found the American arrogance amusing, if no less appalling. "President Knight assured me—"

"The trillion dollars lent to Russia did not come from President Knight's pocket. It came out of the pockets of every man, woman, and child in America. My obligation, Sir, is to see that their money is repaid to them."

"And it will be, Mr. President. Russia is committed to that. But we can't repay it under the current terms."

"Yes, you can, President Kostroma. We know exactly what you have in your Treasury."

Did they? Kostroma thought. Of course, they did, as his government was secure in its knowledge of America's finances—might as well take it all as a given. "Those funds, I'm afraid, have been diverted."

"Competent management of your economy would not have allowed that to have happened when you were under obligations."

"What does competence have to do with drought, Sir? What does competence have to do with earthquakes and epidemics?"

"I cannot answer for Nature, President Kostroma. I can only pray to He who can."

"Yes, our priests have spent much time in prayer."

"And have you, Sir?"

President Kostroma knew that the President of the United States knew he was not a religious man, not even an amorphously spiritual man. A retro Commie-atheist, he had been called by some who opposed him both back home and abroad. An apostate, others called him, who wanted to be nicer about it. And Kostroma was well aware of President Powell's homegrown and very individualistic spiritual position. Somewhere on the right hand of God, it was joked about in America by those who opposed the president or just wanted to get a laugh. To others, of course, it was not a joke, not something to laugh about—only to celebrate. So, President Kostroma had been prepared for the subject to come up, even if it came up light as a feather.

President Kostroma smiled. "I am on American soil. Let me be like a good American and not have my personal beliefs questioned."

A slice of silence, rather cold to the touch, ran through all present, then returned to Kostroma, who dismissed it.

"President Powell, in my first term, I tried to restore the democracy and true and fair capitalism the Russian Federation had had for its first brief life. I have done this not without resistance. I face an election in three weeks. If you place this burden on me, it will fuel Nikolai Zinovy's strenuous and vicious propaganda. He leads an opposition that hates America almost as much as they hate me."

"Well, Sergei, I would like to see you win that election. In fact, we have organized a wonderful event for tomorrow that I think will help. Just for you, I called in my campaign people to organize it. The world press coverage will be great. And your media, my people assure me, are all on board."

Kostroma chuckled. This man was so amusing. "Thank you, Mr. President. Such an honor to be gifted with your greatest American resource."

America had so many resources in its exceptionalism that Thomas wondered which one Kostroma referred to, "What is that?"

"Marketing."

There was a beat of time, a moment of not quite getting the implied criticism, which Thomas was emerging from when he heard the now ancient sound of a cash register—KA-CHING! KA-CHING! Thomas looked towards the sound, and there he saw impish Tommy standing on the table between the couches in good ol' American big-box-store garb behind a counter and at a microphone. "UH, COULD I HAVE A PRICE CHECK ON THE RUSSIAN KOSTROMA DOLL!?" The imp amplified and echoed as he held up a classic Russian nesting doll with Kostroma's face.

Thomas could not keep the gasp at bay.

John Sayers saw the twist his president's face took and stood up quickly to block him from the view of the others. "Excuse me, Mr. President, but perhaps this is a good time to take a break. We have refreshments in the dining room."

"But no vodka, Sergei, sorry, only good American whisky, a man's drink!" said President Ulysses S. Grant from his portrait on the wall by the alcove bookcase somewhat behind Kostroma but well in Thomas's view …

For the first time, President Kostroma was taken a bit aback. Trying to look beyond Sayers, he addressed the president: "What did you say?"

Thomas, looking around Sayers, looked to Kostroma. "I'm sorry?"

"What was that you said about vodka and whisky?"

Thomas stood up. "You heard that?"

Kostroma stood as well. "You said it?"

"No! No, of course not. But I heard it too."

The rest in the Oval Office had no idea what the hell the two presidents were talking about.

"Heard what, Sir?" Sayers asked.

"John, no one should have a TV playing outside this office."

"TV?"

"I clearly heard some ad on TV. President Kostroma heard it too. It was some ad for whisky or something. Or, uh, a radio. Maybe somebody is playing the radio. Check it out." Thomas turned to President Kostroma and gestured an invitation to move to the dining room. "Shall we?"

State visits require State banquets. They are highly ceremonial, minutely controlled, dutiful breakings of bread and mastication of gourmet food. They are formal occasions for informal conversations. Outsiders invited to one could not help but be awed. Insiders could not help but find them routine.

"Well," the First Lady said as she and the president returned to their residence that night after the banquet in honor of the Kostromas, "as glittering state functions go—that one was sure was a bore."

Thomas heard Kathryn's voice but did not note the words. He had words of his own conveniently at hand. "You were beautiful."

"Thank you, honey. How do you know? You weren't completely there."

Thomas sighed. He hoped this was not the preamble to a more prolonged complaint: "It was a long day, Kathryn, of difficult negotiations."

"Not from what I hear."

"What do you mean?"

"There were no negotiations. You just laid down the law to Kostroma."

"As you were not there, how would you know that?"

"Thomas, when have I ever not known what was happening with you?"

"Be that as it may—"

"Be that as it may, many presidents have had difficult negotiations during many summits, but they still managed to be bright and cheerful hosts for the evening festivities."

"I guess I'm just not a bright and cheerful person."

"You can be when you want to be, Thomas. This is the President of Russia; couldn't you have managed to laugh at his jokes?"

"They were stupid."

"I have never known a politician's jokes not to be, but what does that have to do with it?"

"Kathryn, I will thank you to let me be the president of the United States."

"Don't pull that on me, honey. I knew you when you were Barney Fife. And where did you get that dialog? From some old movie? And why didn't you dance with Mrs. Kostroma?"

"I only dance with you."

"You only dance one dance with me and always only a slow one."

"I don't like to dance, you know that. Besides, she wanted me to boogie."

"To boogie?"

"And to woogie as well, I assume."

"It was a swing band, Thomas, classic American music during a period when America and Russia were allies. There was very well-thought-out symbolism there."

"I would like to undress and get ready for bed now."

"Oh no, this is the only time I can get an audience with you. What about the Literacy Conference?"

"Can we talk about this tomorrow?"

"No."

There always came that time when avoidance was no longer possible when the trigger had to be pulled, and when the dirty deed had to be done. "I am afraid I will not be able to fulfill President Knight's commitment to speak."

It was to be disbelieved, and yet it was easy to believe; it was obvious, yet Kathryn had been oblivious to its possibility. "And why not?"

"It conflicts with my keynote address at the Values and Virtues Convention."

"Stanley James," the First Lady enunciated both the given and the surname as if they were in a catalog of vile human body odors.

"The American Morality Congress, yes, it is an important event."

Kathryn Powell was a practical woman, a strong and self-confident (some called it hard-headed) woman who, while having all the proper healthy emotions, never let them loose for public viewing and certainly never exploited them for any agenda of her own. While the hurt she now felt was a genuine reaction, the expression on her face as she sat on a chair, not to mention the verge of tears that reaction engendered, was a somewhat surprising display that Thomas had rarely seen. "How could you do this to me?"

It was not a frivolous question and sharp in its urgent demand for an answer. Thomas tried his best to do so. "These are important people to me."

"Thank you. I guess I'm not."

"Kathryn, I love you more than life, but you are only one vote."

"I am *not* your constituent, Thomas. I am your wife."

"No, in this case, you are the organizer of the Literacy Conference, and that is who I am having to disappoint, with regret."

"President Knight—"

"President Knight is no longer president," Thomas said as he headed for the adjoining bathroom. "But that's a good thought." Thomas walked in, raising his voice so it would now carry out to the bedroom, "Why don't you get President Knight to address your conference?"

"You know George is still in seclusion with the girls." Kathryn amplified back her answer.

"*Yes, he's as good as dead,*" projected from the bathroom.

Kathryn was used to Thomas's sometimes-indiscreet comments, but this one was … "What!" She did not try to tamp down her shock and dismay.

Thomas leaped out of the bathroom as if being chased. "I did not say that!"

"That was an awful thing to say!"

"I *did not* say that!" the president insisted.

"Thomas, I heard you! I heard you as if you were standing right here."

The president walked to their bed and sat down. Sweat began to bead on his forehead. "Look, I haven't been feeling well all day."

Thomas suddenly looked horrible: pale, sweat-drenched, short of breath. Kathryn could see something serious happening, so she rushed to her husband and sat beside him. "Honey, what's wrong? I'll call the doctor."

"No!" No one else, Thomas was thinking, no one else should see him this way. "It—you know—it could just be—I mean, I was thrown into this job so quick. I had to be strong so fast. I never did give myself time to … Maybe, I don't know, maybe I am just feeling it now."

Kathryn took his hand, which was unusually cold, and looked into his eyes, eyes she knew so well, and yet, now, there was something strange there. "You never want to admit you're susceptible to pressure and stress. You always try to hide it."

Usually, Thomas would debate such a statement, but there was no use in doing it now. "Yes, sure, that is probably it."

"Look, why don't you go get ready for bed? Then I will give you one of my patented back rubs you enjoy."

Thomas looked at his wife—not just at her face, not just into her eyes, but at her essence, usually more known than seen. But this night, he could "see" her essence. "I would like that," Thomas most sincerely said, then kissed his wife, finding comfort, warmth, and something to hold onto.

Kathryn's back rubs had always relaxed Thomas. Her technique was not particularly fine; her knowledge of back muscles was non-existent; she just rubbed—this way, then that way, up, down, across to the right, then across to the left. She did not have magic fingers, but they were *her* fingers. It was *her* touch. It was the warmth of *her* hands. The fact that they were being dedicated out of love to Thomas' well-being must have been what made them so effective.

He fell into a deep sleep. Kathryn, feeling better herself, followed him to bed. Soon, the two were slightly snoring in unison.

Thomas slept for several hours. No dreams came to him worth mentioning here, and none woke him. But he did awake suddenly and sharp in perception. There was a leak of illumination coming from somewhere. Thomas raised himself and found the source. Someone had left the bathroom light on.

Night light. He suddenly remembered that he had always needed a night light as a child to keep the monsters at bay, to keep them not under his bed but in his closet. That was always where his monsters resided. The only things under his bed were dust bunnies.

Being no longer a child, he did not need a night light, so he got up to turn the light in the bathroom off.

When he looked in, he was not startled, and no longer surprised, to see his homunculus standing on top of the clothes hamper, wearing a miniature copy of his pajamas. Thomas sighed and sat on the closed toilet lid, directly across from the hamper, as if to silently say, "Well, you called this meeting …"

"Boy, was that childish!" The little imp in the little PJs said.

It pissed the president off. "You! You made me say that!"

"Mmmm, maybe. But *you* were thinking it."

"But I did not say it!"

"Well, anyway, that's not what I meant."

"What?"

"I was talking about your meeting with President Kostroma."

"The meeting with Kostroma? Childish? How could that be perceived as childish?"

Yeah, how?

It was Tommy's voice, and yet Tommy had not said it. Thomas looked around and saw nothing, and Tommy looked around and saw nothing. They were joined together in annoyed perplexity.

It wasn't childishness, Thomas, came the voice again as another Tommy, this one in red PJs and little red horns on his little head, rose from the clothes hamper—where things were soiled and often had a sour scent—to stand next to the Tommy that Thomas had gotten used to. "That was strong, decisive leadership!" The Devil Tommy said, finishing his thought.

There was umbrage to take, and Tommy took his fill. He turned to his more-imp-than-thyself and shouted, "Leadership? Why, it was nothing less than a diplomatic version of going," Tommy crossed his pointing fingers and stroked them off, "*shame, shame, shame!* It was the three-piece-suit equivalent of going, *nah-nah-nah-nah-nahhhh-nah!*"

Devil Tommy stuck a finger up into the air and declared, as Edward Everett might have, as William Jennings Bryan might have, "It was holding the fort! It was staying the course!"

Thomas stood and turned to the bathroom mirror. "It is like a demented cartoon," he told himself, "A truly looney tune." He turned on the tap, bent over to douse his face, then stopped mid-douse. "Why? It did not help last time." He stood straight and tall and looked directly into his own eyes. "This is me," he assured himself, "I am in charge of me."

Devil Tommy jumped up to land on Thomas's left shoulder. With an angel's halo and fancy feathered wings, Tommy jumped up to land on his right shoulder and said in a musical and oh-so-sweet voice, "Thomas, the tree that does not bend breaks."

"Oh, yeah?" Devil Tommy said in a rasping, wise guy's voice. "Mr. President, the tree that does not bend stands tall!"

Tommy turned to his counterpoint. "You know—you're standing on a slippery slope."

"Slippery slope?" Devil Tommy questioned.

"Did I say slope? I meant soap!"

Tommy pointed to the other's feet, and a big bar of soap appeared under them, sliding the hellish homunculus right off Thomas's shoulder. "*Ya-ho-ho-ho-weeeeeeeeeeeee!*" came the somewhat goofy sound, then a quick, unplanned descent.

Tommy chuckled with delight. "He-he-he, I love slapstick."

Flames and all the fiends of Hell shot up behind Thomas, led by a monstrous and hotly upset Devil Tommy.

"*AAAAAAAAAAAAAHHHHHHHHH!!!!!!!!!!!!!!!*" Tommy screamed and then faded to nothing at all.

The president turned the tap back on and doused his head in cold running water.

The flames and the fiends all subsided. But Devil Tommy, triumphant, remained and was there on Thomas's right shoulder when he rose back up, his head dripping water. "Don't worry, Mr. President, I won't desert you," Devil Tommy said as he zipped into Thomas's ear with a small slurp of sound ending in a most delicate *pop!*

The inside of the head of the president of the United States was much like the inside of any other human on Earth. It mainly was the brain, composed of grey matter—eighty-six billion nerve cells—and white matter—billions of nerve fibers. As a command center, which is what the brain is, it was not efficiently designed for the occupation of a homunculus on a mission. Devil Tommy found himself all tangled up in nerve fibers, getting minor burns from firing nerve cells. "Ouch! Ouch! And ouch once more! What a mess! I can't work in conditions like this!"

Devil Tommy snapped his fingers and created a clean white and chrome command center for himself. A magnificent command chair was dead center, looking towards two giant oval screens. Proud of his work, Devil Tommy became just plain Tommy, now in an elaborate military uniform abundant with military regalia, and sat straight and commanding in this seat of command.

"I am here, in the cranium, and I am in command!"

It is a truth rarely denied that sleep is a restorative. Most life on Earth, certainly most mammal life (whoever wondered, indeed whoever cared, if insects sleep?), truly enjoy a sound slumber, much-needed shuteye, and a relaxing snooze. Uninterrupted sleep is an unadulterated pleasure despite its slight resemblance to death. But interrupted sleep, adulterated sleep, sleep violated by awareness, is always a deep disappointment to the sleeper—and often of some concern to the sleeper's bedmate, if bedmate there is.

Kathryn awoke to the light coming from the bathroom, then its death as Thomas emerged and returned to the bedroom.

"Thomas, my God, you look worse than before. Come back to bed, come here."

Thomas did so, crawling into bed and into Kathryn's waiting arms. She soothed him, held him, and ushered him back into sleep.

9

The voice came from beyond.

How are you doing?

It echoed inside the cranium of Thomas P. Powell, the president of the United States of America. It was enough to slightly disturb the sleeping homunculus sitting slumped in the command chair but not enough to wake him. It may seem strange that an inner demon—often the cause of sleeplessness—would need sleep itself. But then, why not? Inner demons may even take vacations occasionally, requiring some deep downtime after working hard, denying downtime to the object of their deviltry. So, as the sounds of a military band playing and a gathering crowd milling invaded Thomas P. Powell's consciousness, the homunculus slept on. It was not, of course, the sleep of the innocent. Nor—it hardly needs to be mentioned—that of the innocuous. Instead, it was the sleep of the insidious.

On the two oval view screens before the command chair, the First Lady, who had whispered the question, would have been seen by the imp if his dereliction of duty had not prevented it.

Fine. I am feeling okay. The answer came from the president.

Feeling presidential? Kathryn asked with a smile edged with concern.

One hundred percent!

Tommy gave a little snort of a snore and moved slightly in his seat but remained happily, we assume, asleep.

Then the world exploded in a booming voice: *LADIES AND GENTLEMEN, THE PRESIDENT OF THE UNITED STATES.* Then, the boom was replaced with "Hail to the Chief," played with military aggression.

"What? Uh? What?" The imp fell out of the white and chrome command chair and flat on his face.

It was a grand and glorious day at Cape Canaveral. The sky was a brilliant blue with just a few well-designed, fluffy white clouds floating in it. The air was moving about in a slight breeze and was crisp with a tolerable coolness. It gave the rays from the sun unimpeded passage to illuminate with sharp definition all that surrounded, especially the newly minted, astonishingly tall, and powerful rocket that sat behind them on a launch pad that had seen many fine leaps into space. The breeze ticked the flags of two nations and NASA, and, on occasion, they seemed to laugh out loud with delight, declaring that it was an "All's right with the world" kind of day.

Thomas felt that. He saw that Kathryn and Charles were feeling it as well. He could see that those on the speaker's platform with him, both American and Russian, were feeling it. As he looked out at the NASA personnel and guests in the audience, he knew everyone shared the feeling. Never had he felt so good when beginning a speech.

"Thank you, thank you," the president said to the crowd, acknowledging the applause. "We are standing on such a historic site. From this site, humanity leaped high, reached for, and touched the moon! Armstrong, Aldrin, Collins, and those who followed went there for noble reasons. And unfortunately—history tells us—for reasons which may not have been so noble. We got to the moon, possibly years before we should have because we were in a so-called 'space race' with the former Union of Soviet Socialist Republics, with whom we were in a so-called 'cold war.' We saw the USSR as an adversary in that race. At least, we did so politically. But did the rocket scientists, engineers, and astronauts see them as adversaries in that race? Maybe they saw them, more appropriately, as competitors in a goal that all humankind had dreamed of for millennia.

"But now we have a new goal—Mars. It is a goal not spurred on by the need to win a race but by the desire to explore and extend the human reach into the stars.

"And this time, the Russian Federation will not be our adversaries, competitors, but partners."

A burst of enthusiastic and sincere applause stopped Thomas for a moment, a moment he allowed the crowd to have.

"And I would like to say that this great effort, which has been a dream for many, is now to become a reality largely due to the commitment and strong leadership of President Sergei Kostroma of Russia."

Hands beat hands, vocal cords vibrated, and the crisp, cool, clear air seemed to respond with a perceivable intensification of all those fine attributes.

"All right, Thomas, my boy," said the little homunculus back in command in the president's head, "You're doing good, following the script. But, now let's see what other scripts might be lying about?"

An imp-size stack of presidential papers, reports, and briefs suddenly appeared off to the side, and Tommy went over to them, quickly looking at and rejecting the one at the top, then the next, one, then the next one: "Nope! Nope! Nope!" Finally, he became bright with the warm glow of a little boy finding a booger. "Ah, this is the one!"

RUSSIA, A CURRENT ASSESSMENT: A SPECIAL REPORT FOR THE PRESIDENT OF THE UNITED STATES BY THE AMERICAN MORALITY CONGRESS read the title page.

Tommy thumbed through the report. "Ah, such clarity of thought! Such wisdom! Such punctuation!"

Tommy slammed the report shut, and it disappeared between his closed hands. When he opened them, a thumb drive with the Presidential Seal rested on his palms. Tommy took it to the command center and inserted it in a slot that appeared before him.

The president had brought Kostroma up to stand by the podium to share in the applause and revel in the cheers. They held hands and held them high—like candidates on the campaign trail—and both men smiled the big, broad, assembly-line-manufactured politician's smile that usually came packaged with glad hands.

Suddenly, Thomas stopped smiling as his head did an almost imperceptible jerk. A new smile appeared on his face, an unusual smile for Thomas, if not for a short creature of his acquaintance. With Kostroma standing slightly off his side, the president started to speak again.

"What a great thing this will be for Russia and the Russian people. It's about time they got their heads into the stars and their feet out of the muck."

A collective, primarily mental *"Huh?"* passed through the moment as people with questioning eyes glanced at anyone they thought might have the answer.

"I mean, Sergei, pal, buddy." the American president turned towards the Russian president. "What is wrong with your people? A more degenerate nation I have never seen. I mean, not only is vodka mother's milk to you people ..." Sergei Kostroma turned to his wife, wondering if she was hearing what he was hearing, "... but you're practically being run by a mafia. Without Eliot Ness anywhere in sight! And prostitution! Jeez, not only is it prevalent in the major cities, the small towns, and down on the farm, but you even have ladies of the night in Chornobyl, where they don't stand under streetlamps—they are the streetlamps! And Sergei, really, half of your pregnancies end in abortion? And your suicide rate, Sergei, that is a hell of a black mark, ain't it? I mean, does every Russian think he's living inside a damn Dostoevsky novel? But this is what comes from a nation without values and virtues. Oh yes, I know, you have reinstated those onion churches with the guys with the ratty beards, which is acceptable for the tourist trade, but come on, get serious! So, this is great. Going to Mars will give your people a goal to reach for and something to lift their spirits—instead of *lifting* spirits. Get it—*lifting spirits*? I mean *to your lips.* Get it? And look, we are here to help you reach that goal. But the first thing you have got to do, the best help we can offer you, is to advise you to start thinking like good Americans. Yes, that would work! Be like us, Sergei, and you cannot go wrong!

"Don't you all agree?" The president asked the crowd with a big smile.

Although open mouths abounded among the crowd—not one sound issued from them.

But sounds came out of almost everyone else in the world. Sounds broadcasted and cabled, beamed by satellite, and streamed, often, but not always, accompanied by faces to go with the sound.

The first of any fundamental importance was Presidential Press Secretary Eric Burton:

"Well, I—you know—I feel, I think—uh—certainly the president of the United States—uh—has the right of—uh—free speech, just like anyone else...."

And then there were pundits on news programs whose opinions were ostensibly educated, informed, and well-considered:

"It was not only unbecoming of the leader of this nation, but it was also rude; it was uncalled for and an insult to a major nation of proud people," said one pundit on one show at three thirty-five and twenty-six seconds.

"Who is your heart bleeding for? Drunks, prostitutes, abortionists, and the criminal element?" answered his competitor on that show at three thirty-five and thirty-six seconds.

Stanley James, president of the American Morality Congress, was interviewed on the subject here and there and, it seemed, almost everywhere:

"I think we can refer to this as the New Candor. Honesty is, after all, one of the great American values and virtues, sadly lacking though it might be in recent public life. President Powell, being a great leader, is leading us here. I say, let us follow, let the New Candor spread throughout the land."

Long-time professional interpreters of the news and the events the news chronicled—often called commentators—did not hesitate to comment:

"One nation simply does not slap another nation's face and expect no consequences. What those consequences will be cannot yet be divined. But does anyone doubt those consequences might be catastrophic in this less-than-secure world? We call upon cool heads to prevail. We are just not sure where those cool heads are."

And those slapped sounded out about President Powell and the country he led. Some, like Nikolai Zinovy, campaigning to gain power in the Russian Federation, were more than delighted to do so, haranguing a crowd ripe for the haranguing:

"POMPOUS!   PATERNALISTIC!   ARROGANT! IMPERIALISTIC!"

And in radio stations and podcast dining rooms or converted bedrooms and basements, lips flapped into state-of-the-art microphones like spasmodic worms making violent love, sending in sounds that eventually came out of speakers and headphones and earbuds in instruments of various sizes in cars, kitchens, workplaces, bedrooms, and home offices that were the hubs of individual egos:

"Yeah, Tommy baby, give it to 'em! Hey, scratch a Russian; you get a Commie underneath! That square is still called 'Red,' you know!

That nation is still an Evil Empire! You're my man, Tommy baby! Talk about a Defender of the Faith! Talk about a defender of our great American values and virtues!"

Generically, it was all news. And it made news, as newscaster after newspaper after news websites reported:

"And today, the president's approval rating dramatically changed—it is up by twenty-two points."

Press Secretary Eric Burton faced once again faces he was so familiar with. Some were friends; some he detested; some he had a hard time reading; some were old professional colleagues; some he had an understanding with, and some he found more than attractive. But all he was now delighted to face and say:

"The New Candor: I think the people like it!"

And on the primary Sunday morning interview show, the Secretary of State, Herman Berger, was asked:

"Mr. Secretary, can you explain the New Candor?"

"Well, it's nothing arcane. It's just simple honesty with the international community. The American people, you know, hold not only this president but also this government to a high standard of moral leadership. After decades of, shall we say, less-than-honorable individuals occupying the White House and less-than-totally-forthright government agencies, the American people are demanding this. I think they find the New Candor refreshing."

And somewhere, the ever-present Stanley James was looking straight into camera number two and declared:

"Thank God for Thomas P. Powell and his strong, decisive leadership."

Former President George Knight saw none of the pundits, reports, spokespersons, or videos and heard none of the screeches or cheers. In his grief for his wife and in his daily and nightly efforts for his daughters' recovery, he had shut out the reported-upon world of politics and governance that had once been the world he had occupied and, more importantly, the world that had occupied him. He did not read newspapers, he never turned on the radio, and the only thing he watched on television with any abandonment were old movies, preferably black-and-white ones, and several cable channels dedicated to TV series he had known and loved as a youth, especially the sitcoms, especially the, quite frankly, low-comedy ones, the silly, slapstick ones.

He was, indeed, making a list of series and even individual episodes that he desperately wanted to show Lisa and Molly, for he knew they would like—even love—them and would laugh at them wildly, even as young as they were. To hear them laugh again—that was the only goal of his life.

He spent much time in the girls' room, which had been converted into a hospital room equipped with the latest in high-tech aids for monitoring the girls, both still in comas. Each girl had her special bed, of course, and he usually sat between them in his old, favorite easy chair, brought up from the den where it had been for twenty-six years. When there was nothing he could do specifically for the round-the-clock nurses (he often made their lunches or dinners, spoiling them for future on-duty meals), and if he wasn't in his bedroom sleeping or watching old sitcoms, he would sit in this easy chair and read books. Histories, often on arcane subjects, biographies on obscure individuals, and twentieth-century American novels that the modern reader had abandoned—Dos Pasos and Farrow and Marquand. He liked to feel that he had adopted them and was keeping them alive.

Patricia Whitmore, his long-time secretary, looked after President Knight. She knew him as well as any person did, knew his needs and wants, and quietly ensured they were fulfilled. His chief-of-staff, who had only worked for him during his presidency but had become fiercely loyal, looked in on him often and tried to engage him with news of the outside world.

"Don't care, Jerry," President Knight had said. "Not until the girls are fully recovered. And possibly not even then. Oddly, I'm enjoying this cocoon."

But one day, Jerry left him a *Time* magazine. It had a cover story on "The New Candor," which Jerry felt was a fair and comprehensive report on its meaning and potential effects.

George Knight did not want it, but Jerry had left it on a side table, and he found himself drawn to it. He took it, sat, and read. He was halfway through, shaking his head, mostly metaphorically, but once or twice in actuality, until one of the girls moaned and seemed to stir. George Knight got up quickly and went to Molly, who was stirring.

The *Time* magazine fell from his lap and onto the floor.

Finding the actual tank took them a while, but they had. At least they reported that they had, and who could argue with them as who else knew? They had found it abandoned in a field in a neighboring country that once had been a part of the USSR and, for an awful, violent time, had been under the "protection" of the Russian Federation. But that time was over, and the tank was old, but it had been "the" tank, the one that another Russian politician had stood on to raise himself higher in his fellow Russians' estimation. Now, brought back to Moscow and cleaned up, it served as the perfect Red Square platform for Nikolai Zinovy.

"President Kostroma has given us nothing but weak, indecisive leadership," the handsome in a blunt way, serious in an urgent way, man of height and heft and humorlessness said to the shoulder-to-shoulder crowd before him and millions beyond him reached by the wave of electronic signals. "This was well demonstrated by his standing there on a world stage and allowing the president of the United States to lecture him, to shame him, to shame the Russian people. Kostroma does not deserve another term as president of our great land. He does not deserve more years to suck the strong life's blood out of our glorious federation. Grant me the privilege, though, and I promise that I will, from my own veins, give Russia a transfusion of our ancestors' good, strong blood through a boldness that will shock the world!"

10

Children are notoriously fickle in the love of their toys. Had Charlie's Maximan—he of the loose right arm—been real and not just the plastic dream of a feature film incarnation of a thin, comics page hero, he might have felt lonely and ignored and raging with jealousy over his abandonment, his relegation to the edge of a bookcase shelf from where he could see Charlie and his new, non-heroic companion: a strange pink, purple, and worse, plush, vaguely mammalian-like creature. But Maximan was only a petroleum-based entity shaped into a pleasingly recognizable form, not a feeling creature of any sensitivity. It was meaningless whether he was just an image on a shelf or an object of imaginative play. And yet, somewhere in the vast stretch of reality, there was a sadness, unfelt though it may have been. But reality was vast enough for reversals, and Charlie's Maximan may be called back into action one more. It was, at least, a hope to hang onto. Until then, though, the world belonged to the pink, the purple, and the plush.

"You have to be quiet, Racky," Charlie said to his currently closest companion as he, holding the raccoon tight, climbed out of his bed, intending to see what was happening in all the bright illumination of the nighttime adult world that was determined to keep him in the dark. He slipped on his slippers, slipped on his robe, and then slipped out of his bedroom and into the center hall. His mother was in one room talking to others; his father was in another talking to other others. Charlie silently sought Racky's opinion of which way to go. They conferred for a second or two, then made a mutual decision, influenced by Racky's love for the man who had brought him into this world.

The four governors from four states from four corners of the nation were pleased to have gotten a meeting with the president, delayed, put off, rescheduled, and moved though it had been over several months. Thomas met them in the early evening in his private sitting room in the family residence to make it up to them. He could offer them hospitality in a warm room and not just reception in a cold one—the cold he reserved for his position.

"Mr. President," Governor One said. "I agree. The economy is doing very well, which makes many people happy. Wall Street's happy. The Fortune 500 is happy. The banks are happy. The hedge funds are happy. But, in my state, I have many, many two-income, even three-income families who can't make it into the middle class. So, they aren't particularly happy."

"Children are starving in my state," Mr. President," Governor Two added. "And it's not just for food. Some are starving for affection because both of their parents aren't around because they are always working. And they can't even get paid leave when their children are sick."

"But," the president responded, after a moment's reflection, "the operative word is, *some?*"

The implication was clear, and the governors were uncomfortable with it being so—*as long as it was not "all," then all was pretty much right with the world.*

"I love your New Candor, Thomas," said Governor Three, who had been in the House with the president, served on committees with him, and shared gym time with him. "May I practice it? Your laissez-faire is more like a laser blast at the middle class and the disadvantaged of this country—and it's just not fair."

The president was impressed. "Bob, is this a hint that you will be in the running to succeed me? That sure sounds like election rhetoric to me."

"Doesn't make it any less true."

"Well, that's for the people to decide. Listen, gentlemen, you are governors of states elected to manage the affairs of those states. That is a great task that takes bold, sometimes unpopular actions. But it is your task to do, not mine. So please do it. Manage your states. Do you really want to go back to Big-Daddy Federal government? Are you so childlike as to need a nanny?"

Governor Four had a profound distaste for Thomas and had said little at the request of the other three, but she felt a point had to be made. "We understand, Mr. President, that the Federal government can't do everything. But does that mean that it should do nothing?"

"People are hurting out there," Governor Two emphasized.

"I'm aware of that," the president said. "I'm not insensitive to it. But I believe the virtue of patience is called for. Do you doubt that our good economy will eventually bring everyone along?"

"I thought the trickle-down theory died a long time ago," Governor Four said, questioning Thomas's thinking.

Thomas liked this woman no more than she liked him. "You know, Nancy, trickle-down is not important. I'm interested in trickle-up. If the people of this country will have self-reliance, self-discipline, self-control, self-respect, and embrace the values and virtues instituted by our Founding Fathers, then that will trickle up in our society, and then, maybe—"

"BOO!"

A pink and purple monster had arisen from behind the president's wing-back chair, as unexpected as mortality, and the "BOO!" had bounced all five executives out of their skins for a second, and slightly out of their seats, except for Bob, who fell entirely out of his. Charlie found this delightful and funny, laughing while shouting, "I scared you! I scared you!"

All then was a chaotic mix of movements, talk, and hearts pulling back from the beating speed they had suddenly achieved as Thomas angrily grabbed his laughing son, and three governors rushed to uplift the fourth, laughing himself.

"CHARLES! What do you think you are doing?"

"Are you alright?"

"Yes, I'm fine."

"Charles, how often have I told you not to do that? Now look what you have caused."

"It's fine, Mr. President. My little girl does the same thing."

"It's a phase, you know, it's one of those phases kids go through."

"You got us good, Charlie."

"What are you doing here? Where is your mother?"

"She's with those people. I'm supposed to be in bed."

"Yes, you are supposed to be in bed. I will call your mother and—"

"No! You take me and Racky back."

"Why don't you, Thomas," Bob said. "I think we have taken up enough of your time."

"Yes, well, maybe that's a good idea. I do have dinner guests waiting. I want to thank you all for coming and sharing your thoughts," the president said as he shook each gubernatorial hand.

As the governors left, two tousled Charlie's hair with genuine affection.

Thomas picked up his son so he could stand tall and be stern. "Charles, I am very angry with you."

Charlie did not see his father as stern or even hear it in his voice. He liked being up here, level with his daddy, seeing his face up close, seeing even the slight stubble on his cheeks. Charlie had always been fascinated by the stubble on his father's face when it was there. But he also liked running his hand across his daddy's cheek when it was not. And anyway, it was play. He held up the pink and purple raccoon to his father's face and declared, "It was Racky's idea."

Thomas pushed the North American native away from his face as he carried his son back to his bedroom. He put his child under the covers and tucked those covers around him.

"Charles, it was naughty of you to have left your bedroom after your mother had—"

"But you did not come to say good night to me yet."

"Charles, you know I always come in to say good night to you."

"But sometimes I'm asleep, so I don't know it."

"Well, I know, but still, you know that I never go to bed myself without first coming in to kiss you good night."

"Make Racky talk."

"Not tonight.

"*Pleaseeeeee!*"

"No, Charles, I'm late for my dinner. Now go to sleep. I love you; I will see you in the morning."

"No, you won't."

"What do you mean?"

"Mommy says you'll leave before I wake up."

"Oh, that's right, well, when I get back then, good night."

Thomas leaned down and kissed Charlie on his forehead. Often, Charlie would grab his father's face by the cheeks and pull him down to his lips so he could kiss him back on his daddy's lips, but not tonight.

It had almost become a routine, and Thomas was disturbed by its absence.

After the president left the room, turning the light off as he exited, Charlie turned to his raccoon and wiped a small tear on his face onto Racky's. Racky did not complain and, indeed, consoled the child. "Hey, that's okay, Charlie," Racky said tenderly, "I can talk without him." That made Charlie smile. He gave Racky a big hug, then settled down to sleep.

There was a slight chill in the family dining room where Stanley James, his wife Beth, and Kathryn Powell sat eating their salads. There was nothing wrong with the White House environmental controls. The chill emanated from something less susceptible to mere physics.

"Literacy?" Beth James asked as if the concept and reality were not something she was intimately aware of, and so she was confused by its mention.

"Yes," the First Lady answered. "It was an assignment President Knight had given me. Our convention starts tomorrow as well."

"Oh," Beth James said, beautifully expressing disappointment, her talent coming from much practice. "I was so looking forward to having you with us and—"

"Sorry I'm late," the president said as he entered the dining room and took his seat. Darren, the butler, immediately served him his salad, and Kathryn was instantly relieved.

"Well, Mr. President, how did the meeting with the governors go?"

"You know, Stanley, it is a harsh business giving people the facts of life."

"Yes, it is a hard task. You have only the best intentions, the best wishes—"

"Stanley has always faced that problem," Beth said with the natural compassion she had always had for her husband. "From the time the American Morality Congress was not much more than just him and me."

"That's right, I'm afraid," Stanley James said, smiling at his wife and the memory she had conveniently brought forth. "The message has always had its appeal, of course, among certain people. But other people haven't wanted to hear that it is *they* who must change, and not the world. But they are taking more and more to the message. Thanks, I must say, in no small measure, to yourself, Mr. President."

"I have always felt that moral leadership is the finest service we can aspire to in public life. But we all need guides, Stanley, and you have served well as one for me."

Finding the mutual admiration society too thick to wade through, Kathryn stood abruptly with a quick pushback of her chair. "I think I need to go check on Charlie."

"I was just with Charles. Do you know what he did? He left his bedroom and snuck into my meeting with the governors and gave us a bit of a fright with this 'suddenly yelling Boo thing' he's been doing lately."

"Boo thing?" Stanley James had to question.

"Yes, sneaking up on you and jumping at you and screaming, Boo!"

"How strange," Stanley said, and Beth nodded in agreement.

"Your child left his bedroom after being put to bed?" Beth James asked, quite sincerely, as if this was the first incident of its kind in history.

Kathryn had a quick image of a stucco wall, Beth's face, and the scraping of the one upon the other. "Charlie is a child of initiative."

"Initiative?" Beth said, and Kathryn wondered if it was the concept or the word itself that Stanley's strongest supporter did not understand.

"You know what? I should have a talk with Charlie. I'll be back for coffee and dessert."

Darren entered with an attention-grabbing urgency and whispered in the president's ear.

"Yes, fine, send him in," Thomas instructed. Then, to Stanley and Beth, he explained, "The Secretary of State needs a moment."

When Herman Berger entered, he did not bother with a preamble. "Mr. President, a coup is currently underway in Russia."

"What do you mean a coup?" The idea itself was surreal. Although Thomas was getting used to some surrealness in his life, this was too out of phase with his smooth view of the unfolding of the near future. "They're having their election today."

"The election did not go well," Berger said. It's still too close to call, but that may not matter. Nikolai Zinovy seems to have the military behind him. He's in Red Square right now, standing on top of that damn tank again."

Thomas said nothing, knowing it was a moment to reflect.

Stanley James could have said much, and his wife, Beth, would have backed him up like a well-armed militia, but instinctively he knew it was not his place. Intellectually, of course, he hated that fact.

The First Lady, whose wit Thomas had always found amusing if he did not always appreciate it, knew exactly what to say. "I think the Russians have just canceled their debt to us."

11

Nikolai Zinovy liked elevation. He liked it in thought, only considering the most serious of ideas. He liked it in ideals, only adapting those which gave him cause to think the most profound thoughts. He liked it in art; high art was the only art for him. He liked it in sex. He had very high standards for the beauty of his partners. And he liked it in his position in life: the higher, the better, the highest, the best. He was now giddy with a less conceptual and more material elevation. He was enjoying standing on the famous tank in the famous Red Square. It placed him well above the crowd below, the perfect place to bask in the cheering patriotic spirit. He turned to his partner in current events, General Zinkoff, and, with a smile, said, "I assume you have no problems re-targeting our Topol missiles?"

General Zinkoff, in an imposing uniform proudly burdened with a chest full of ribbons and medals, inquired, "Are there any particular targets?"

"Major cities in America. With one reserved to go straight down the big mouth gullet of President Thomas P. Powell."

"That would be very precise targeting. But we will manage."

Zinovy broadened his smile. Zinkoff smiled himself, joining Zinovy in pleasant, joyful camaraderie.

For the president of the United States, almost any day can bring about a "situation," a thing, an emergency, a crisis that demands not only the attention of the chief executive but of those highly qualified— it is hoped—often highly political—it is tolerated—men and women who advise the president. It was good that President Kennedy created the Situation Room in the West Wing of the White House, where they could all gather and communicate with the world and get real-time information. And it was a doubly good thing that it was constantly being upgraded so that such communication and information was of the highest quality possible. It was a location that could not help but be dramatic, and dramatic it now was. Crowded along the long conference table were dark-suited advisors, uniformed masters of military tactics, and Herman Berger and John Sayers. Clustered along the wall were advisors to these advisors. Most monitored voices in their earpieces. And, of course, at the head of the table was Thomas P. Powell, once a cop concerned that auto-encased citizens signaled before turning right or left. Now, the president of the United States, whose signals could mean a turn securing the future—or a turn destroying it. If this weighed heavily on Thomas, as might be expected, he refused to show it. That, he felt, was part of the job—to be calm in the middle of the storm, just as a straight and even tie was part of being well dressed.

Herman Berger, just off the phone, turned to the president. "Mr. President, I have a report that the prime minister of Russia has officially disbanded the Federal Assembly."

An advisor at the other end of the conference table shouted, "I have confirmation of that. All members are being ordered to quit the building."

An advisor in a chair along the wall, with a laptop on his lap from which he had just received information, announced it. "Mr. President, the Mayor of Moscow has just thrown her support behind Zinovy."

A general, off to the side, on a cell phone: "Mr. President! President Kostroma has been taken into custody by the Russian army and—" He paid attention to a small voice in his ear. "And—yes—it's been confirmed that the Russian nuclear codes have been taken from him."

"Okay, I'm getting official word here that the Russian military has placed themselves under the command of Zinovy."

"Kostroma is being called an enemy of the people, and demands for his execution are coming in. Zinovy has refused but says Kostroma will be tried."

"General Zinkoff has just put the Russian armed forces on a full state of alert, especially on their Western border. They are prepared, he is saying, to defend the homeland from forces within or without."

General Reardon, the Chairman of the Joint Chiefs of Staff, a man in fine physical shape, a man enjoying admirable good health, a man who only spoke when what he had to say was urgent or wise or well-considered or deeply troubling, now spoke: "Mr. President." His words hushed all others; his bearing demanded a cessation of activity. Attention was directed to and concentrated on the general. "Our man at the Russian military HQ has confirmed it. They have re-targeted their ICBMs. Their rail-mobile missiles have been taken out of the garrison. They have fourteen strategic aircraft in the air. They have two to three hundred protected warheads now aimed at us."

Did anyone in the Situation Room feel a penetration of cold? From a source that was non-living and non-caring? Possibly, but professionalism would have abated it.

"Protected?" The president asked.

"Invulnerable to our attack," General Reardon answered. "But we have sixteen hundred invulnerable to their attack."

"And their targets?"

"Major cities. Especially ones with port activity. And Washington, of course. Since we have the bigger club, it's where they can hurt us the most. Cut off the head; the body will flail."

"Ah, the New Candor!" was gleefully shouted and heard by only Thomas. He closed his eyes, turned his head toward the shout, opened his eyes, and, as expected, saw Tommy "Imp" Homunculus, in tiny glory, wearing a glorified military uniform dripping with metals, standing in the center of the highly polished conference table. "What a refreshing change in global politics!"

As if to confirm this, General Reardon said, "Zinovy is a complete wild card, possibly a madman. And he now has access to existential destruction. I think we ought to consider striking first."

"Wow! Talk about a hot-button issue!" Tommy said to his audience of one.

"General, you're kidding me," said the president to history.

"I am not, Mr. President. We have the B61-11."

"Which is, again?"

"It's an earth penetrator. We developed it in 1995, and it's been improved lately. It burrows up to twenty feet into the ground before it detonates. Zinovy will go to Chekhov, their underground command post about forty miles south of Moscow. We can hit him there. We'll send over about seventy B61-11s and jellify him and the command staff."

"Cut off the head; the body will flail! Cut off the head; the body will flail!" The imp pranced and chanted in the center of the table.

"So, you would not hit Moscow?" The Commander-in-Chief asked while commanding composure within himself.

"No, Sir, radiation drift will make it uninhabitable for generations, of course, but—"

"Thank you, General. I will give it some thought."

"Think of all those glowing prostitutes!" Tommy took delight in the image.

"Sir, I advise you—"

"I got it, General."

"This is a volatile situation, Mr. President, and—"

"Yes, General, it is."

"Ah, cheer up, Thomas!" The imp was all smiles. "*Armageddon* excited! Aren't you?"

12

They had been in the Situation Room since nine the night before. Now, at three thirty in the afternoon, after a stretch of no news (which did not mean it was good news) from Russia, a quiet had invaded the room, and the president of the United States was beginning to nod off. General Reardon noticed this and, concerned that his Commander-in-Chief should not be seen "asleep at the wheel," and possibly a bit of compassion for the man, he addressed him quietly, "Mr. President?"

Light bringing color and awareness expanded Thomas's consciousness, and he knew immediately who was talking to him and the possibilities that might be presented. "Yes, General, any developments?"

"No, Sir, it is now two thirty in the morning in Moscow. It's all quiet over there. I suggest you go upstairs and get some sleep."

"Sleep?"

John Sayers approached them. "It's a good idea, Mr. President. You've been here for over sixteen hours. I've cleared your schedule, of course."

Schedule? There had been something significant on the schedule. Thomas thought briefly, seeking, then knew. "The AMC convention?"

"Sidney James has moved you to the last day. He says his prayers are that you will be able to make it."

"Good, okay, and I assume there's no need to run into the bunker."

"Our people in Moscow tell us no," the general said. "We think Zinovy was just showing off his big, um, tool to impress us. Like chimps do, you know."

"Well, General, I wasn't unimpressed."

"Ours is bigger, Sir," the general assured.

"And engorged?" Sayers asked.

"It's in a high state of readiness, I would say, Mr. Sayers."

Thomas did not like these slightly suggestive metaphors and, turning to Secretary of State Berger, moved beyond them. "How are our diplomatic communications?"

"Ambassador Wallace is scheduled to see Zinovy—unofficially, of course—in six hours. Eight-thirty a.m. their time. He will strongly protest the takeover as an illegal action, of course. But then, once that formality is over, Wallace will see if we can do business with the man."

"Is there nothing we can do—outside of 'jellifying' Zinovy—to get Kostroma back in power?"

"Why bother?" Berger was blunt enough to state. "Zinovy now has the nukes and our money. He is now the man to deal with. Kostroma just kept arguing with us."

"Re-targeting their nuclear weapons at us is a pretty strong argument, Herman."

"No, Mr. President," the general said, "that's not an argument, that is a fight. Not men around a table, men with clubs."

"And ours is bigger," Thomas stated, possibly seeking assurance and comfort.

"And Zinovy damn well knows it. You want to talk, talk with your club in your hand."

"All our phone calls from here have been completely rebuffed, sir," Berger said. It's really in Wallace's hands. So, there's nothing more you can do right now. Sleep is your best option. You will want to be well-rested when decisions must be made."

"Yes, all right. But you will—"

"Of course, Mr. President."

Thomas began to leave, then stopped. "Do you think Zinovy is stalling?" he asked Berger.

"What for?"

"To lull us into a sense of security," the general answered. "Maybe he's hoping we will think we can do business with him, bringing our guard down. And then, boom! He hits us."

"Destroying the world?" The president asked.

"Maybe to a reactionary nut like him, it's just an adjustment. Maybe he thinks it would be good to decrease the surplus population. But we can take advantage of the lull ourselves. A strategic strike against his bunker. Then we won't have to worry about whether we can do business with him."

"General—"

"It's my duty to give you options, Sir."

"I appreciate that, General. But I haven't heard of any *options* from you, just one."

"Maybe one is all Zinovy is giving us."

"Maybe, General. In any case, your other advice to get some rest, I can take and appreciate."

Kathryn, who had delayed her arrival at the Literacy Conference—officially, because of a cold—had insisted that Thomas shower first and get into clean pajamas. He did, emerging from the bathroom clean and minimally relaxed as Kathryn drew the curtains closed.

"I feel like I've been sent home from school with a fever," he said as he crawled into bed.

"Enjoy the luxury."

"Yes."

But there was the luxury of thought as well. "Kathryn, what have I—"

"Shh! Now's not the time; just get some sleep so you can be rested to deal with matters at hand. Monday morning is soon enough to analyze the game."

"A sports metaphor?"

"The politician's best friend, my dad used to say. Short, simple, easily understood."

"He was a hell," Thomas said in the middle of a yawn, "a hell of a public servant."

"Yes, he knew how to get those streets paved."

"You should wake me in—"

"I'll let you sleep as long as possible."

"But—"

"Would you like me to get in bed with you?"

"It's too early for you to sleep."

"Not to nap. You know how much I've always liked afternoon naps. And how often do I get the chance? Give me a moment. I'll be back soon." She left for the bathroom as Thomas fell asleep.

The president's sleep was deep and undisturbed by dreams. Kathryn lay awake for quite some time, worry not going away. Eventually, she, too, fell asleep. Neither knew that the curtains were now open despite Kathryn having closed them. But the pad-pad of little feet and the near-silent rustle of covers as something small climbed into the bed had the power to bring Thomas to a lightly awake state.

"Charles, what are you doing? You should be in your own bed," Thomas said as he turned to face his child.

But it was not his child. It was a pink and purple horror who smiled maniacally and said, "Give us a kiss!"

Thomas screamed and grabbed the stuffed animal, throwing it across the room. Then, he leaped out of the bed as if a horrible pink and purple slime had been left behind.

"Thomas, what?" Kathryn said in confusion as the door to their bedroom swung swiftly open, letting in a bright light. General Reardon, John Sayers, Herman Berger, and a ridiculously tall and broad Marine carrying the nuclear briefcase or "football"—another sports metaphor—followed.

"Mr. President! The Russians have launched missiles!" the General announced.

"What!?"

"At least fifty heading for our major cities," Berger added.

"Mommy!" Charlie came running into the room, scared. Kathryn, out of bed, swept him up into her arms.

The Marine placed the "football" on the bed and opened it up. Inside was nothing but one big, brilliantly red button.

"Now, Mr. President!" the general, so used to giving orders, ordered the president. "We need authorization now! We must strike back!"

"Wait a minute!" Thomas yelled, grabbing his head, which seemed ready to explode, and then his chest, which was preparing to follow suit.

To quiet the moment, Herman Berger said softly and sadly, "It has been confirmed, Mr. President."

"The fucking Russians are trying to wipe us out!" General Reardon made clear.

"Any countermeasures?" the president asked.

"Of course, of course, they're in play. But some are going to get through. We've got to attack back! Now, now! PUSH THE BUTTON NOW!"

Thomas leaped to the red button and pushed it down hard.

"Missiles away!" The general yelled with some hint of glee just as a big, muscular missile appeared in the sky over Washington. "My God, first strike, the bastards got in the first strike!"

The general raised his fist in defiance. As if in answer, the Russian missile became all light and energy and force, soon taking the shape of a vibrant mushroom, sending out a visible, fiery wave of destruction, flattening all the great monuments of America, bursting into the room through the windows, disintegrating the general with his fist still raised. Thomas turned to Kathryn and Charlie; Charlie held his arms out to Thomas as he and his mother became nothing but light—then only dust.

"*NOOOOOO!!!!!!!!!!*"

Thomas's scream became the essence of white, then the silence of death, and then the dull whistle of wind blowing over nothing—absolutely nothing.

13

The desolation was near complete, near enough to give credence to clichés. It *was* "like a war zone." For it was a war zone—if mutually assured destruction could be called a war and not just "a momentary, yet eternal in effect, lack of good judgment." And the landscape *could* have been described as "like a moonscape." But Buzz Aldrin would not have found anything magnificent in this desolation. It was the skeletons of famous structures and buildings surrounding, with a horrible hot wind breezing through them; the husks of vehicles that once gleefully rolled on wheels, tooled around, transported, sped, and occasionally parked so that copulation (uncomfortable yet oddly satisfying) could be accomplished in; and the shadows of the once-living now branded on the sides of broken concrete and the once-imposing marble—it was all of this that framed the desolation as more malignant than magnificent. It was also the shattered, disjointed reality that saw the skeletons of the famous buildings and monuments moved and arranged weirdly in a Stonehenge circle around the deconstructed White House sitting precisely in the middle.

Thomas P. Powell, president of the United States, or former president of the United States, or president of the former United States, stood in the center of the devastated remains of the White House, dressed still in his pajamas (unbelievably crisp and clean they were), a perfect look of horror and terror on his face as disbelief flooded his brain.

Besides the sound of a hot, dry wind, Thomas perceived the moist sound of quiet sobbing. He turned around and saw standing there among the rubble the horrible homunculus, the inhuman creature that should have been ugly but looked too much like Thomas for that. He was also in pajamas identical to Thomas's and just as crisp and clean. He held and hugged the charred remains of Racky the Raccoon. "Poor Racky," he wailed. "Poor, poor Racky."

Anger, atomic in nature, blew up in Thomas. "Poor Racky? What the hell have you done?"

The imp's eyes went saucer round, and, in all innocence, he queried, "Meeee?"

The conversation did not need to be continued. The situation, though, needed to be assessed. Thomas looked around him, turning a full three hundred and sixty degrees, once slowly, a few times quickly. Then he stopped and looked at himself. He concentrated on his right arm. He grabbed it. He pinched it and squeezed and felt both actions as well and painfully as he should have. Still, it had to be asked: "Am I dead?"

"Ummmmmmmm—could be! The world certainly seems to be, in any case."

"I—I don't understand."

"Destiny, maybe we are talking here about destiny."

It was not destiny but a sudden empty void that Thomas was feeling. "Kathryn? Charles?"

"And billions of others."

"I—I will never see them again."

"Oh, I don't know about that."

"What, what do you mean?"

"Depends on how nice you are to me."

"I could kill you!"

"Well, that's not nice."

"Where is Kathryn and Charles?"

"Well, they are not here, are they? There is no one here but us Toms!"

"You said—

"I said nothing."

"You intimated—"

"Like a good politician."

"That I could see Kathryn and Charles."

"Depends on how nice you are to me."

"I don't know what you—look, I promise not to be *not* nice to you."

"Oh, my goodness, a compromise! That's unusual for you."

What energy Thomas had drained from his limbs, what breath he had exhausted from his lungs. He staggered over to the imp and fell to his knees before him, coming face-to-face, eye-to-eye. "Please, can you take me to my wife and child?"

"Well, let's see, I could take you back to before the big boom and *show* them to you."

"You could?"

"Yeah, sure. I know you want to see them one last time and say goodbye, which is perfectly understandable. They won't be able to see and hear you, but I could do that."

"Who—what—who are you?"

"Ehhhh, maybe I'm your travel agent. Look!"

A craft appeared before them, fading up into solidity, floating ten feet from the ground. It was a strange hybrid of a flying vehicle. Its front half was a slick and sharp, needle-nosed silver rocket and the back half was an ornate futuristic Victorian dirigible. Heinlein led the way, and Verne brought up the rear.

Thomas looked up at it in astonished awe. "What is that?"

"It's a ship. Not a ship of state, I'm sorry to say. But I can't give you everything. And anyway, Mr. President, YOU BLEW THAT! He-he-he," Tommy chuckled in self-amusement. "No, it's just a ship. But it travels through time and travels through space. It can be big …"

The ship suddenly grew to enormous proportions, shadowing the world and felling Thomas like a tree to timber down, flat on his back.

"Or it can be very small."

The ship rapidly reduced to the size of a pea, falling into the imp's open hand. He took it over to Thomas, who had sat himself up and presented it to him.

"See. But no matter what size, it is your ticket to seeing your wife and child one last time. Plus a few other things that I may show you at the discretion of my good taste."

It was the invitation of a devil; Thomas was sure of that. He stood up, suspicious of the endeavor. "Ah, well, maybe—"

"Hey!" Tommy threw the pea ship up into the air. It expanded to its original size and then came to rest before them, an entrance opening in its side. "You want to see Kathryn and Charlie? One—last—time? Get in!"

The command was as swift and sharp as the kick in the ass the imp—suddenly as tall as Thomas—gave the president, propelling him through the air, through the entrance, and into the interior of the hybrid ship.

14

When Thomas stood up inside the ship, he noticed that the imp had become a weirdly tall little boy, as tall as the adult him but as childlike in visage and proportion as Thomas must have been when he had been a child. Thomas felt as if he was leaning, seeing the imp at an angle, yet also from the rear, from below, and from above, all at the same time. His face must have formed—possibly for real, surreally—into a question mark, for the imp was quick to explain,

"Hey! I'm tired of getting a crick in my neck looking up at you, all right? Plus, who could look up at you now, you death incarnate, you destroyer of worlds, right? So—you ready?"

Before Thomas could answer the insult or the question, the ship's interior, which had been the essence of nondescript, turned into a round room with its circle walls providing a 360-degree view of what was happening outside. Two cushy and comfortable swiveling armchairs popped up under Thomas and Tommy, gathering them in inoffensive hugs. The chairs had minds of their own (or possibly it was Tommy's) and swiveled them as the chairs saw fit—to the right, to the left, around and around—to present before their eyes what needed to be before their eyes.

A receding, expansive view of a scorched Earth slammed into Thomas's retinas. It was all fires and destruction and burnt vegetation, all covered by the swirling closeness of the irradiated fog of a massive cloud that enfolded the ship until the ship broke free into blinding sunlight, until the Earth became a complete sphere, dwindling, dwindling, surrounded by the black of reality pin-pricked by the glow of burning stars still energetic, still "alive" unlike the scorched Earth below.

There was a quiet, a stillness, a sense of the universe abiding in its billions-of-years majesty.

"Look at that," the strange, out-of-synch doppelganger said. "Even when you guys destroy your world, the universe doesn't even notice."

Then, a button appeared and floated before Tommy, and he gleefully pushed it. "Going down!"

"AAAAAAAAHHHHHHHH!!!!!!!!!!!!!!!!!" Thomas screamed as the ship fell with a speed his mind tracked as his body felt every inch, foot, and mile as if they were skidding themselves over him. The view was a chaos of closeness expanding, growing, ready to slap him flat.

Then, the ship stopped on a dime in mid-air. It was a vast, floating, old, corroded Roosevelt dime with tarnishing a prominent blemish on FDR's face.

Beyond the floating-dime landing pad was an urban street of crumbling and burnt-out buildings, useless vehicles, and a few people still living (some solace in that, Thomas could not help but think), damaged and dark souls shambling along. "My God!" Thomas said. "Did the bomb do this?"

Tommy laughed. "No, you idiot, this is just normal urban blight. Those are people of Hispanic and African descent, not charred white people!" And then he laughed again.

"Oh," Thomas said, the embarrassment a cold shaft that penetrated.

"Never came here on a campaign stop, huh?"

"Well—it was not really an issue we—"

"But the personal morality of politicians and people was?" Tommy questioned as the dime floated closer to the scene. "Oh, look! Someone is being self-reliant."

An armed robber sped out of a check-cashing store with a full paper bag as an alarm started blaring, alarming no one except Thomas, "You call armed robbery self-reliance?"

"Well, at least he didn't ask the government for a handout. But you're right; he's a bad guy, and it's too late for him. Now, of course, if his kids could get a leg up … But, well, won't it be great when the bomb hits here? Problem solved!"

"You say the worst things."

"What? What? At least the bomb will make it a level playing field."

The hybrid ship rose from the dime, turned to find a direction, and zipped back into the sky.

Blue became cloud became black became a multitude of looming colors. There was purple and white and straw and red and gold and apple-cheek. It was hard at first for Thomas to see what was before the ship, but finally, some focus was pulled out of the air. He could see that it was a monumental porcelain figurine of a round-faced—and thus cute as all get-out—little girl of red, curly hair, wearing an oversized purple dress with white flowers and a straw hat, obviously her mother's, carrying her mother's gold-colored purse as well, her little finger up to her mouth pointing out her innocence. On its base were the words: TIME TO PLAY DRESS UP. It was one of the most frightening things Thomas had ever seen.

"Damn it!" A voice came booming to shake the ship. "You've got a mouthful of rotten teeth!"

The 360-degree view rotated before Thomas's eyes, speeding the cute monster away and replacing her with a broad and deep view of a suburban middle-class—or possibly a bit lower than that—living room with furniture cared for yet worn, a carpet vacuumed yet stained, and a few framed pictures on the wall of landscapes and flowers. Two giants occupied the room. A late-middle-aged man in jeans and a plain, cream-colored, short-sleeved work shirt with a logo on the pocket, and a woman with short gray hair, squarish in build, angelic in face, wearing some service uniform.

Where the hell...? Thomas thought.

"Iowa," Captain Tommy said as if he was reading Thomas's mind, or was Thomas's mind, or controlled Thomas's mind, or at least didn't mind Thomas's mind.

"Iowa?"

"It's a nice, if dowdy, little neighborhood. Maybe some bad elements are moving in, which worries Mr. Benson there. Mrs. Benson is wonderfully oblivious to it."

"But—but they are—giants."

"No, we're gnats. That's 'gnats,' not 'nuts,' the president of the United States can't be nuts; that would just be weird, wouldn't it? No, we're just tiny-winy little specks in a ship the size of two motes and a few dead human skin cells, resting on a Maplewood knick-knack shelf with a nick in one side and a knack for gathering dust."

"Why...?"

"Shut up. I want to listen."

Mrs. Benson took a bag of frozen peas away from her right cheek and smiled at her husband, a man often more concerned about her than himself. "But I *can't* give up my job, Jack."

"But if you don't, we can't qualify for the state's dental benefits. Your income puts us over the limit."

"But we need the money."

"It helps, sure, Honey. But you also don't need to be in so much pain. And what you make isn't enough to pay for the dental work ourselves. It's one of those catch things?"

"Catch things?"

"You know—It's a number."

"What?"

"A number—Catch, uh, some number."

"22."

"That's it! We're stuck in that as long as you work. We can't afford the cost of all the dental work you need."

"Well, it won't cost us a thing because I just won't have any dental work done."

"Oh, sure, that's the smart thing to do."

"Well, what am I supposed to do? I like my job."

"As a caregiver? What is that but a glorified slave."

"What's wrong with getting paid to help somebody?"

"Nothing, it's getting underpaid for it. That's the problem. Look, Honey, why don't you just quit? We'll get on State medical, have your dental work done, and then you can go back to work."

Thomas was appalled, *appalled*! There was the problem right there before him—people with no values. Cheaters were gaming the system, giving up honest work to suck funds from other people—asking for a free ride to a free lunch.

"Mr. President," the imp said with a smile, knowing intimately what Thomas was thinking. "You don't have to worry about it anymore. The Bensons are dead now—fried to a crisp and blown away like so much dust. Oddly, some of Mrs. Benson's rotten teeth survived."

Mrs. Benson was appalled as well. "But if I quit, there's no telling who Mrs. Anderson would wind up with. You know, some of the other caregivers, it's just a job to them; they aren't always the nicest—"

"So, you should sacrifice yourself for an old lady who's going to be dead in a couple of years anyway?"

"Oh, it won't take that long," Tall Tommy said. "She's now but a puff of radiated dust."

"Jack!"

Jack Benson, a factory worker, good at his job—when he had a job—disappointed in some aspects of life (his hometown team rarely won; his one child died young; fancy coffees irritated him), had never been disappointed in his wife. She was the air he breathed, the music he listened to. He went over to her and enveloped her in a much-practiced hug. "Well, I'm sorry. But look, I hate seeing you in pain."

"I will be fine—I will be fine, just as long as they make frozen peas," Mrs. Benson said as she smiled and hugged her man back.

Tommy was smiling as well as he turned to Thomas. "Teeth!" he said, then began to spit most of his out in a vaudeville routine of dainty and delicate decorum. Finished, he smiled at Thomas again, then turned that smile into a most effective toothless grin. "Woo nees em?"

The two-toned ship lurched as it rose off the knick-knack shelf, positioned itself to blast off towards a screened, open window, and kicked Thomas back into his chair as it moved with minimal caution towards the expanding-metal-grid pattern of the screen, diminutive enough to make it through one of the open squares. Then, it chased light itself to get away.

"Away" was eventually mid-sky, where the ship took a stationary position, and Tommy leaned back in his chair and announced that he thought he would take a little nap.

"What? No! I want to see Kathryn and Charles! Now!"

"Really? Now? In your mood? You're pretty depressed, you know."

"Well, who's been showing me depressing stuff?"

"I'm just taking you where the atomic wind blows."

"What the hell does that mean?"

"I don't know. You tell me. You're the grown-up."

"Kathryn and Charles—now!"

"Not before we lighten your mood. Let's go have some fun."

"Fun? My world's been destroyed. I'm in some purgatory—"

"Or hell!"

"Or—" Thomas stopped. Was that a possibility? "Okay, or Hell. And you want me to have fun?"

"Okay! Okay! Would you like to see something happy?"

"I would be *happy* to see my wife and child!"

"I'll tell you what, I'll tell you what—let's compromise. I'll show you some children."

"If you take me to some damn orphanage, I swear, I don't know how I'll do it, but I will kill you!"

Tommy just smiled his particularly sanity-slicing smile, and the ship dropped from the sky, and Thomas was thrown straight up to smack and splat flat against the ceiling.

The ship burst out of the *Time* magazine cover in former President Knight's hands and shot up to stop and position its small self mid-air for a good view of the girls' unfortunate hospital-like room. It was the *Time* with The New Candor cover and the time when the exhausted father of Lisa and Molly, who lay in dual comas in dual beds, was reading reluctantly about his successor. "Thomas, what the hell are you doing?" he quietly asked as he shook his head.

Thomas had a quick and sharp stab of offense before a little girl's moan pulled it out.

George Knight dropped the magazine on the floor and went to his daughter. "Lisa, Honey, it's Daddy. Can you hear me? Honey? Lisa?"

Lisa moaned in an acknowledgment of consciousness returning and perceiving the world again. Her little body moved under the blankets, and her eyes slowly opened to find the face of her Daddy. "Daddy, I'm thirsty," came a quiet, little whisper. But it was as loud as a cheer to the father.

"Okay, Honey. I'll get you water, I'll just—"

"Lisa? Daddy, I hear Lisa."

George Knight spun around. She was not wrong; it was not an illusion; his other daughter was awake and moving. "Molly? Molly?"

"Can I have some water too?"

George Knight fought the urge to cry with relief and the desire to laugh with joy, for there was a job to do, needs to fulfill, and tasks to perform. "Nurse!" he called out through the bedroom door. "Nurse!"

Tommy turned to Thomas. "Were you happy for them?"

"Yes, yes, of course I was."

"Or was your first thought, 'Oh, shit, maybe he'll want his job back'?"

A red flare burned in Thomas's eyes as he instantly prepared to jump on the imp, ready to strangle, when the 360 view became nothing but a white glare, and Thomas fell out of his chair and onto a floor made up of bad, unexpressed thoughts.

The glare diminished and left a close-up view of snow—cold, sparkling in the sun, packed snow. The view then receded, widening the information Thomas received about where he was now, facing a vast, heavens-piercing mountain.

"Denali!" the giant homunculus announced. "The tallest mountain on the North American continent! Used to belong to Russia, you know. Used to be part of a folly. Used to be named Mt. McKinley. Used to be the President. McKinley, not the mountain. Remember him? No one remembers him. No one will remember you—because there will be no one left to remember." Tommy laughed a deep, low laugh that soon ascended in pitch until, as a shriek of lousy humor, it forced Thomas to cover his ears and squint his eyes to keep things out, maybe to keep things in. Then the shriek stopped dead, leaving behind a silence just as dead—until Tommy spoke again. "Actually, that's not 100% true. A few members of your species will be left with burns on their bodies, radiation in their flesh, and a curse on their lips. It will be a new vulgarity—the worst of the worst. Never just said, but spat out. *Powell,* they'll say when they want to be profane. *Powell,* they'll say when they want to threaten. *Powell,* they'll say when they want to bemoan their fate."

"Shut up!" Thomas commanded.

"Shut up? Me? Asking me to shut up is like asking the sun not to shine, the moon not to change phases, and the bladder not to fill and empty on a regular basis. But I get your point. I promised you fun, and here I am, being a pre-post-apocalyptic downer. So, let's go skiing!"

"What?"

There was a sound, a buzz, then the hum of mechanics, followed by a clunking of metal fitting into place.

"What was that?" Thomas asked.

"Just the ship's skis lowering and locking," Tommy said as the ship sped to the top of the mountain, landing on the peak, affording a peek down the mountainside.

Vertigo and nausea hit Thomas in his head and stomach. "No, no, let's not do this."

"Oh, come on, *merde de parti.* It'll be fun!"

With its slick retro-future front and ornate future-retro rear, the ship tipped downward. And downward it slid into a high-speed mountain descent, weaving, banking, and going around outcroppings of boulders in near misses. It flew off the edge of a cliff to land on a slope and continued down. Then Thomas could see trees, beautiful columns of slamming, smashing death coming towards them.

It was the most frightening experience of Thomas's life, and he wanted to scream eternally.

Then, between two heartbeats, it became the most fun experience of Thomas's life, and he wanted to laugh forever.

And indeed, when they came to rest at the bottom, he was still laughing — a gleeful, crazy laugh that Tommy watched with some interest.

Finally, Tommy said, "Look back up the mountain." The 360-degree view accommodated as Thomas did so. Denali, formerly named after a former president, towered above in majestic wonder, with bright, white clouds seemingly attached to its peak like huge flags. "You know, right after you help blow up the world, it will become the world's biggest nightlight!"

Thomas stopped laughing.

"Off we go!" the imp declared. The ship shot through the air, the 360-degree view blurred, and Thomas was pushed back into his chair.

Soon, they slowed to a more reasonable speed, skimming along an ocean's surface, joining a pod of dolphins that jumped out then arched back into the sea as if they were musical notes sounding, fingers tapping a tattoo, incarnate joy leaping again—again—again.

And again, Thomas began to laugh. Not at the dolphins or with them but at his delight and giddiness. "Wow! Wow! I would love to show Charles this!"

"Oh, yeah," said the only "child" available, "that would be great. Why, if *Charles* was here, we could play PINOCCHIO!"

"What? Why would we want to—"

"Look!"

Thomas looked—then screamed like a little girl banshee.

A giant blue whale came right at them and opened its mouth as the shrinking distance between it and the ship compressed light and sea and spray until all there was left was dark in the belly of the beast and a wave-rocking rest as the ship-now-boat bobbed in the digesting fluid of the whale's stomach.

"Quick, go out and start a fire," Tommy said.

"What? I'm not going out there."

"Haven't you ever seen the film? It's the only way to get out of here. *Charles* has it on DVD, you know."

"Well, I meant to watch it with him, but ..."

"But what?"

"I do *not* like cartoons."

"It's not a cartoon, you fool! It's a classic! Now go out there and start a fire."

"With what?"

"Oh, yeah, okay, alternate route!"

The ship rose and shrank and passed through flesh and into the lungs just as the whale surfaced to exhale. The ship was shot out of the blowhole into a light quickly dimmed by condensation in the spout until it shot out of it, grew to its normal size (if anything about this ship was normal), and settled mid-air to watch the beast swim away.

Despite the fright of it all, Thomas noted the majesty of the great creature receding and turned to Tommy, struck with the idea that they should follow it. But the imp was in a contemplative, wondering mood, hand on chin, brow pinched.

"But would *Charles*," Tommy began to question, "really want to play Pinocchio? No! He's a modern kid, up-to-date, and a fully fine consumer of the latest must-have. *Charles* would want to play Maximan and Valquar!"

The correctness of this, the absolute, undeniable correctness of the imp's assessment, hit Thomas like a giddy tickle. "Yes! Yes, he—"

Valquar, larger than life, practically larger than the blue whale, looking precisely like the hand-held toy Thomas had several times repaired, popped up into the 360-view and yelled out, "BOO!" Not what you would expect from a master of evil, but then this giant Valquar looked just like Charlie ...

Thomas fell back, grabbed his chest, and landed in his chair. "Oh my God!"

"Valquar is your god?" The imp impishly asked, "How weird."

Valquar Charlie grabbed the flying ship, which was no larger than a beach ball to him, and—as super-villains were wont to do—announced his plan. "I will crush you like an egg!"

"No, Charles—Charlie, no!" his father cried.

"Hands off, Valquar," a booming voice pounded the little ship. It was Superhero Maximan, with the visage of Agent Jeff, to the rescue.

Maximan Jeff grabbed Valquar Charlie and forced him to relinquish the ship.

"You interfering fool!" Valquar Charlie said as he broke away and flew to escape.

But Maximan flew after him at much greater speed, caught up to him, tackled him mid-air, and hung on.

"Please, Maximan," Valquar pleaded, but now with the voice of—could it be? Maximan swung Valquar around, and Thomas could see that he now had the face of Kostroma. "A little consideration, a little—" Maximan squeezed tight the torso of Valquar Kostroma, and now suddenly, with the determined face of Herman Berger, said, "Can't play that emotion card with me, Valquar!"

Valquar broke away but did not flee. Instead, he—or she, now that Valquar had the toothless face of Mrs. Benson—pleaded her case. "Peesh, Ma-i-man. All ah wan ish shom nu teesh."

"Nooooo!" Maximan screamed, his mouth becoming the whole of his head until the scream abated, the mouth shrank, and Maximan was now Stanley James. "Not until you learn self-reliance, self-discipline, self-control, self-respect, and embrace the values and virtues of—"

Valquar suddenly grew an eighth-mile, changing from pleading Mrs. Benson to belligerent Nikolai Zinovy. "I'll show you self-reliance!" Valquar Zinovy flew to the hybrid ship, grabbed it, and flung it into space!

The Earth receded farther and farther, the moon came closer and closer, and existential dread bore deeper and deeper into Thomas. It was all made ridiculous when he saw Tommy in a white dinner jacket, cool crooner's microphone in hand, singing, "*Fly me to the moon and let me play among the stars.*"

They were halfway to the moon when Maximan, now with the head of General Reardon, caught up to the ship. "Let's nuke that madman!" He said as he strapped a big, fat H-bomb onto the hybrid ship.

"No!" Thomas tried to command.

"Oh, don't be so weak and indecisive!" the giant Maximan Reardon said as he took the ship into his hands and flung it hard back to Earth."

"*Nooooooooooooooo!!!!!!!!!!!!!!!*"

The ship slammed into the Earth's atmosphere, the slick, needle-nose front heating up, the ornate rear burning up, the H-bomb, now an anthropomorphized cartoon creature, desperately hanging on to what was left.

"Stop it! Damn it! Stop it!" Thomas yelled at Tommy.

"What can I do?" Tommy asked in all insincere sincerity.

"WE *DO NOT* LIKE CARTOONS!" shouted Racky the Raccoon, fifty times his normal size, keeping pace with the falling ship. He grabbed Hydro the H-bomb ("Let me go, let me go," the cartoon carrier of carnage squeaked out) and flung him up and into the sun to join his own kind. Then Racky struck a pose of attention in mid-air, gave a snappy salute, and flew off just as the half-ship dived into the ocean, leaving a plume of steam behind.

The ocean was agitated by this intrusion, but soon it calmed. Then the ship, its truly steam-punked dirigible back half attached again, bobbed to the surface.

Thomas was a mess—physically and mentally. His hair was tousled, and his pajamas were soaked with sweat

On the other hand, Tommy was as cool as a cucumber—as clichés would have it —and was coolly munching on a cucumber when he said to Thomas, "Fancy a trip to Russia?"

Red Square at night: the illuminated architecture of Tsarist Russia dominated, providing the dull light of a romanticized history and the smoldering warmth of false pride to the crowd, a massive crowd of spirited people believing that the voices of the loudspeakers blasting at them from loudspeakers spoke not just to them, but for them. There were signs, posters, and banners with bold, painted words of anger, hate, defiance, and harmful intent. There was frenzy and agitation and a deep desire and dangerous demand for the world to acknowledge that they, these offended Russians, were at the center of the universe.

The hybrid ship appeared amid all this, the size of a tennis ball and invisible to all. It flew among the crowd, among the giant Russians, all bundled up against the cold, their frosted breaths expelling, yet hot despite that. It was more fascinating than frightening to Thomas, as the perspective could not help but be compelling.

Russian, a language that Thomas had always felt was not as harsh and ugly as German, yet not as beautiful and lilting as French, flowed into the ship in a multitude of voices, some amplified, but most intimate if brief, as the hybrid ship flew in and among and past and towards and away from hundreds of individuals.

"What are they talking about?" Thomas asked the imp.

"Oh, all kinds of things, you know. Yeah, for our team, and expressions of pride in their country, and lots and lots of comments about how much they hate you—"

"Hate me?"

"Oh, sure. Look!"

Tommy flew the ship on a straight path through the thick crowd until they reached an opening, a circle formed by the crowd, at the center of which was a hanging figure, an effigy of Thomas. It had been repeatedly spat upon and was, at this moment, being doused with gas and set aflame. Tommy zipped the craft around to show Thomas an outdoor art show of signs and posters and placards featuring him, his face and body, in altered and defamed photos and crude to well-drawn caricatures. He was the devil in one, Hitler in another, a pompous and quite literal ass in a third, and a diminutive crazy-faced Napoleon in a fourth. The multitude of his roles was dizzying: an evil sorcerer, a black-suited cowboy villain, a fierce and ugly black dragon being lanced in the heart by a white knight Zinovy on a white steed—an anthropomorphic turd, which Tommy giggled at.

"You see, right now, at this moment, over here—*you* are Valquar."

Thomas suddenly felt a constriction around his whole body. He looked down, shocked to see he was now suited as the ultimate evil, Valquar. He looked up at the imp, who was impishly—as might be expected— pointing a toy gun at him.

"Bang! Bang! Bang! Bang!" Tommy yelled, then broke into gleeful yet maniacal laughter as the Red Square scene around them melted away and an ornate, nineteenth-century-infused hotel suite was revealed.

The hybrid ship settled right next to a fly on the wall. The fly took no notice.

President Kostroma was sitting in a chair, nervously fingering a coin, a relic of a past Russian president who had taken the state into dictatorship and oppression. It had been a commemorative coin celebrating the grab of land that had previously been part of another country. Etched in metal, in relief, was that president's hard, haughty face. It was an ironic good-luck piece that Kostroma had carried for years—and a reminder that power concentrated into one person was rigid, unbending, and cold.

Two soldiers stood at the door, AKM assault rifles in hand. They were not protectors but guards.

A knock came at the door. The soldiers let in two men that Thomas recognized as having been among Kostroma's contingent in his visit to the White House. The soldiers frisked both men and then allowed them to approach their leader. After greetings and hugs and an offer of water or tea, the three men sat close to each other and conferred in whispers.

Thomas turned to Tommy, desperate to hear and understand what the men were saying.

"Oh! sorry!" Tommy said, snapping his fingers. The men's Russian became English.

"It's unbelievable, Sir," said one of the advisors. "They have bussed people from all over the country to Red Square. There are very few actual Muscovites there."

The second advisor added, "This has obviously been highly planned. This mob is not indicative of the true feelings of the Russian people. I am convinced that most Russians do not want to see a return to dictatorship."

"They are just playing to the camera of the Western media."

"The media manipulation is masterful."

"Zinovy is smart. He hired an American media consultant."

"What about the army?" Kostroma asked his advisors.

"Zinovy has Zinkoff. That's definite; he's been in on it from the beginning. But some of the younger generals, majors, and captains are not happy with this. They want to see democracy finally succeed here."

"But Zinkoff is powerful. He has a tight reign. So, Sergei, what can we do?"

Kostroma sighed at having to state what he had concluded. "I hate to say this, my friends, but there is not much we can do. It is up to the United States. And President Powell, if only he would condemn this illegal action."

"But, Zinovy has the bombs. He's pointed them at the US again. Powell must know that by now. He must tread carefully."

"No!" Kostroma said. "Zinovy is crazy, that is true. But how crazy? If I were Powell, I would call his bluff. But, more importantly, I would get to know the Russian people. Send a message to them —"

"Apologize?"

"Could we expect that?"

Kostroma considered it. It could be so helpful; it could turn the events and stop the craziness, but ..." Kostroma seemed to collapse. "No, no, we cannot expect that."

Thomas saw a man defeated and wondered if he was just that man, that one individual, or if he represented many more—men, women, children—all defeated now.

Thomas turned to his strange yet familiar companion. "I would like to see my wife and child now," he stated quietly with only a slight hope of compliance.

Just as quietly, even kindly, the imp said, "Okay."

The hybrid ship, the front speaking of a future that might never be, the rear speaking of a past that never was, slowly appeared in Charlie's bedroom in the White House. The ship was now the size of a basketball, and so the humans in the room—Charlie in the arms of his mother and his mother in a rocking chair gently rocking Charlie asleep—while still, from Thomas's perspective, far larger than him, they were not larger than life. But they were large with life.

Mother and child were, of course, unaware of the ship. But even if it had not been invisible to them, they may have remained unaware of it, for they sat in a small universe of their own, a mother and child existence, and light did not penetrate from other universes.

"Mommy?" said Charlie, warm, loved, and nearly asleep, but not yet.

"Yes, Honey?"

"How come Daddy don't love me?"

Shock and truth and suspect struck Kathryn. "Charlie!"

Shock and confusion and fear struck Thomas. "No!"

"Charlie, of course, Daddy loves you. He loves you very much. You're the whole world to him. But—well, certain people express their love differently."

"Oh," the sleepy head said.

"So, are you okay? You understand? Daddy loves you very much."

"Uh-uh," Charlie said as he closed his eyes, relieving Kathryn. But slowly, they opened again. "Mommy?"

"Shhh. Go to sleep, Honey."

"If anything bad ever happened to me, like happened to Lisa and Molly, would Daddy quit like Uncle Georgie did?"

"Well, Honey, things would be different because I would be here to care for you. Uncle Georgie lost his wife."

"Well, then, if something bad happened to me and you and you died, would Daddy quit and take care of me?"

Kathryn meant to say the obvious but instead said the only truth she knew: "Well, Charlie, I—I don't know."

Thomas knew. Thomas knew what would have to be. For one does not give up … what? What cannot be given up? Duty? Power? Values? That spot in the center of the universe you had found or forced your way into? The virtues of never ceding any of these? Love? He looked over to Tommy, small again, the homunculus, the imp, the dopey doppelganger, with a smug smile and a bit of a titter tripping off his tongue as he floated in mid-air.

Thomas exploded in anger and smacked the creature hard with a backhand, shooting him swiftly toward the 360-degree view of the mother and child. The imp smashed against the curved view and spattered like a tomato, becoming a mess of body parts slowly dripping down the surface. The eyes were rolling around this way and that; the nose was sniffing out the territory; an arm found a leg, and a leg kicked against the stomach. But the mouth, independent of the head and face, was the most active. "Ehhh, don't get your knickers in an uproar. None of this has been real. I've just been kidding with you! Get it? *Kid-ding.* BOO! HA! HA! HA! HA! HA! HA!"

The mess settled to the ground, and Thomas settled into darkness.

15

Light, just having snuck over the planet's curve, streamed into the president's bedroom through windows revealed by curtains opening seemingly by themselves. The light played over the president's closed eyes, slowly wakening him. He was one of three lumps in the bed. One was Kathryn, serene in sleep, a beauty at rest. Another, smaller, was hidden under the blankets. Thomas gingerly raised the blanket to peek underneath. A pink and purple raccoon face greeted him, but it was part of a whole that Charlie clung to. "Oh, my God, Charlie! Charlie!"

Thomas scooped the child up and brought him out from under the blankets, enfolding him in his arms. He kissed his forehead and cheeks and took delight in Charlie's groggy protest, "Daddy!" But Thomas tickled Charlie, and Charlie laughed and soon knew play was at hand.

"Thomas, what's wrong?" Kathryn had woken, prepared for an emergency, confused by the laughter.

"Nothing! Nothing!" Thomas said as he jumped out of bed, holding Charlie, who was holding Racky. He swung his boy onto his shoulders and exited the bedroom, barefoot and in his pajamas, giving Charlie a thrill ride.

It was quite a sight: the barefoot, pajama-clad president of the United States with his delighted child riding on his shoulders exiting the elevator and making his way down corridors to the Situation Room, entering with great purpose and determination.

Everyone was there, exhausted but alert as their duty demanded.

"I take it Zinovy hasn't sent the missiles over yet?" the president said to his staff.

The scene was surreal enough to hinder tongues. Finally, the Secretary of State, Herman Berger, spoke up. "Uh, no, Mr. President. But—well, we were just about to come and get you. Ambassador

Wallace waited five hours to see Zinovy and was given only five minutes. We aren't quite sure—"

"Noon, nine p.m. in Moscow, I will address a joint session of Congress at noon. Throw it together now. General Reardon, many in the Russian military command do not like what's happening, right? General Zinkoff is only one man. Find those loyal to democracy and the rule of law and get them on the line. Now, right now, General. Secretary Berger, Kostroma may be under house arrest, but his closest advisors are free. Get to them now! And call Ambassador Wallace and tell him that under no circumstances is he to have any more meetings with Zinovy. Who has Russia got in America right now? Their Ambassador? Their UN rep?"

"Yes, Sir," Berger said. "But they're not sure what their status is now with the new administration—"

"There is no new administration in Russia. Is that clear? You call the ambassador and the UN rep and tell them that. In any case, today, they are working for humanity. I've got something for them to do if they want the job. And George Kn—President Knight. I need him. Get him here. I'll be back down in ten minutes. Make those calls. We've got a lot of work to do."

The president then turned and galloped out of the room, giving Charlie the best thrill ride of his life.

The House of Representatives of the United States chamber was smaller than it appeared on television. But then, just about everything was smaller than it appeared on television. This was not just because televisions had grown to Bradbury proportions. It was also true in the early days when the first commercial television sets had diagonal screens no bigger than ten inches. For early television, despite owing its existence to the vacuum tube, did not exist in a vacuum. People had to make sense of this intimate conduit to the broad world outside of the living room. It was a world squeezed for delivery—vacuum packed, shall we say?—then was gathered up and expanded by viewing human imaginations. In their enthusiasm, they may have expanded the world a bit more than necessary. But no one had ever really complained. It had just led to the occasional realization that things were not as big as they appeared on television. It was not a traumatic realization, just a momentary point of interest.

This was what it had been for Thomas when he first entered the House chamber to take his oath of office after he had been appointed to fulfill another's term. And, oddly, it had returned to him every time he had entered the House chamber since. Except for this time. This time, as he entered right after the Sergeant-at-Arms announced: MR. SPEAKER, THE PRESIDENT OF THE UNITED STATES, this time, the chamber seemed huge, monumental. The people gathered—representatives, senators, cabinet members, Supreme Court justices—seemed to be giants of somber expectation. He walked up the center aisle to polite but light applause. No one reached out to shake his hand. He did not shake the hands of the president pro tempore of the Senate nor the Speaker of the House, seated behind and above the Speaker's platform. He gave them a nod of acknowledgment, then turned to face the chamber and what seemed a vast field of fellow humans, most of whom were wondering if he was there to announce war.

Although that chamber seemed to Thomas to be all the world at this moment, he knew it was smaller than that. All the world still existed outside the chamber, and he knew it was jittery with actions, some of which he had put into motion.

President Knight was transported at top speed from the now happy room of his daughters to the White House. He exited the limo and entered the executive mansion with purpose and concern.

An aide handed a cell phone to a Russian general in Moscow.

The Russian Ambassador to the United States rode in his Russian ZiL limo to an American Air Force base and onto the tarmac to stop close to an American fighter jet. He emerged to be greeted by a Major and the jet's ground crew, which outfitted him in a flight suit and helmet for a quick trip to a location he never thought he would be invited to see.

Kostroma's advisors huddled over a computer tablet in a secure location outside of Moscow.

President Knight and the Russian general in Moscow had a frank conversation, the content of which Berger conveyed to Kostroma's advisors.

And Thomas P. Powell, the President of the United States, faced the individuals in the House chamber, the American public, and, indeed, the whole world.

"At this moment," the president began with no preamble, "two hundred to three hundred protected thermonuclear warheads, targeted on American cities, including Washington, stand ready in Russia to be fired at the whim of a man who has no legal, not to mention moral, right to do so. But this fact is not affected by legal and moral concerns. So, for your convenience, Nikolai Zinovy, private citizen of the Russian Federation, I have called together here in this chamber the three branches of the government of the United States of America, not to mention my own family, my wife, Kathryn, and my son, Charles. This chamber, Mr. Zinovy, is not a bunker."

It was a well-made point, and Nikolai Zinovy, sitting in the Chekhov bunker outside of Moscow, watching President Powell on a large screen TV, got it.

"This chamber, Mr. Zinovy, and the human beings within it are our representative government made manifest. If you want to take out the American government—there's no time like now. If you are afraid of retaliation, Mr. Zinovy, don't be. One-half hour ago, I ordered a stand down of all 1600 of our protected thermonuclear warheads, plus every single one of our nuclear devices."

President Knight and the Russian general chit-chatted about inconsequential things while waiting on their phones—their families were asked after, and the benefits of running were agreed upon. Then, their wait was over when the Russian Ambassador joined them on the line from the control room of the US Army Space and Missile Defense Command in Alabama. He was happy to confirm to the Russian general what President Powell declared was true. And he continued to confirm the truth of the president's statements, which all concerned heard from myriad sources.

"In initial response to your re-targeting of missiles onto our cities, we, of course, re-targeted our missiles onto your cities, but I have now changed that order. None of our missiles are currently targeted at any location within the Russian Federation. Not even missiles carrying the B-61-11 penetrator warheads that, I am told, can burrow underground to get to you in your bunker."

Zinovy, in his bunker, shook his head. He did not believe President Powell. He could not believe it. He would not believe it.

"So, Mr. Zinovy, be our guest if you want to blow us up. And truly become evil incarnate. And now, since you do not legally represent the people of Russia, I will no longer talk to you."

In Moscow, a massive crowd of people had gathered outside the American Embassy, attracted by a large screen where the video feed of the president's speech was being projected, with simultaneous captions large enough for even the people in the back of the crowd to read.

"I now wish to address the Russian people directly. If you allow this usurper to send your missiles to rain destruction upon the American people, then you will share in his evil. But I do not believe you will allow it. For I know you are not evil people."

In Red Square, at a series of trucks set up by Apple, Amazon, and others, people clamored to get the free iPads and tablets handed out, playing the president's speech. Through computers, phones, and word-of-mouth, people throughout Russia found ways to see and listen to the president.

"And you never have been."

There was a moment of silence as Thomas paused. He took a breath and began again. "A while back, when I shared a stage with President Kostroma, the true leader of your nation, I said some things about Russia and the Russian people that I now most heartily regret. I cannot explain why I said what I said. It's been chalked up to something called the New Candor. Candor is no excuse for rudeness."

Couples in small apartments saw and listened. Families in rural communities saw and listened.

"I could say that I, momentarily, was having a mental disturbance. But I don't care to fall back on such an excuse. The reality is that what I expressed came from some dark area in my soul."

Russian soldiers in barracks saw and listened.

"It is a dark area that is too frequent in the human creature and ignores the ancient precept of treating people as you would like to be treated. Rather, it gives in to the equally ancient but irrational desire to remake other people in our image."

Shoppers in large department stores and village markets saw and listened.

"And that is a desire not suited to the non-divine. In recognizing this dark area in my soul, I could feel the shame that was my due. But

I cannot erase the words I said. I cannot rewrite history. I can only offer you, the Russian people, my most sincere apology."

Zinovy sat with Zinkoff in their bunker and scoffed at the American president's highly emotional and manipulative words. And they assured each other that those words were meaningless. It was a ruse, in their way, a clever but ultimately ineffective first strike in a psychological war. As they congratulated themselves on recognizing this, a door flew open, and the general, who had of late been conversing with President Knight and the Russian Ambassador to the US, entered with several armed soldiers. Zinovy and Zinkoff were placed under arrest and led out of the room as President Powell, on the TV, said:

"As long as I am the president of the United States and have any powers of persuasion among the legislators of this land, we will commit to do whatever we can to aid the Russian people."

President Kostroma did not hear these words of the American president. Those charged with securing him in house arrest at the hotel had not allowed him to have any contact with the outside world—no computers, no internet, no television, not even the now almost quaint form of radio. His only source of information came from his advisors, and his guards had only allowed them in twice, and the last time was now an uncomfortable distance in the past. Kostroma was a strong man, but it was impossible not to feel fear in the situation surrounding him. Not for himself—he knew the history of his country too well not to have accepted years ago that his life was constantly under threat— but for his wife and children. Though he was a strong man, he had not been strong enough to avoid love, marriage, and the gestation of another generation, given his political activities. His wife, of course, had chosen to join him in his life. But what choice had he given his children, who might now suffer? It was always the children who caused the most profound sadness; it was always the children who were precious. Why? Were they not just going to grow up to become adults? Some of whom would threaten children.

It was the most cynical he had ever allowed himself to be. But given where he was, given the—

There was a knock at the door. One of his guards opened it. An officer of high rank entered and ordered the two guards to leave. Then, he ushered in Kostroma's two advisors. Both were smiling broadly. One carried a bottle of vodka, and the other carried four glasses.

The vodka was poured, toasts were made, and dark cynicism fled the room.

In the American House of Representatives chamber, the Sergeant-at-Arms delivered a note to Thomas at the podium. Thomas read it, a small and brief smile crossing his lips. He then looked out upon the gathered, then into the TV cameras.

"My fellow Americans, my fellow members of the human community: I have just been handed a note that informs me that the Russian Army and proper legal authorities have arrested Nikolai Zinovy and his co-conspirators in his attempted coup. The codes and control of their nuclear arsenal have been recovered and, at this time, are being returned to President Kostroma. I have been assured that he has rescinded the order to target their missiles on America."

The chamber was silent. Having braced for an unimaginable outcome, it was taking a moment to accept the reality of its disappearance. Thomas folded the paper and put it in his breast pocket, dutifully making a mental note to turn it over to the national archives. And then he said to the world, "May I be so bold to speak for everyone when I say—Whew!"

The president's big grin as he wiped his brow set off an uproar of joyful laughter and pounding applause that erupted in the chamber.

Up in the House Gallery, the First Lady was very visibly shedding tears, and Charlie was jumping up and down, up and down, up and down, and yelling, not quite really knowing why. But it caught Thomas's attention, and he called up at his son sharply, "Charles! Charles!"

It stopped his son. Indeed, it stopped the whole of the chamber. Quiet returned, except for Charlie's small but audible voice. "Yes, Daddy?"

"Charles," the president said sternly, "Charlie," the father said gleefully, "now that your father has not helped to blow up the world, he would very much like to tell you that he loves you and that in the future he intends to make that much clearer to you than he may have in the past."

"Okay," Charlie said. "Tell me now."

"I love you, Charlie. Tomorrow let's sneak around the White House and go Boo! at the Marines."

"Okay!"

Laughter returned. Applause returned. And amid it all, the president announced: "Members of Congress, Justices, cabinet members, and distinguished guests, I have the distinct pleasure to introduce President George Knight and the misses Lily and Molly Knight."

The Sergeant-at-Arms opened the door at the rear of the chamber, and President Knight entered carrying his daughters, one in each arm. He was greeted as an old friend, a colleague to emulate, a father to share joy with; many hands reached out to touch him, pat the girls, and thrust thumbs up. Many hardened politicos, tough sons-of-bitches, and bitches, as some thought of them, proved their shared humanity with copious tears and uncontrollable smiles.

The girls were shy and buried their heads into their father's neck, making them even more precious in the eyes of the world.

When the two presidents returned to the White House—Thomas with Kathryn on his arm, Charlie holding his hand, President Knight still carrying his two daughters—they were greeted by the White House and West Wing staff. They all gracefully accepted the applause and cheers. Seeing John Sayers in front of a large group, Thomas called him over.

"John, call Stanley James with my regrets. After all, I've decided to attend the Literacy Conference. We'll go tomorrow. You'd better have a hotel suite booked. And make sure they've got a particularly bouncy bed for Charlie. He likes to bounce, you know. And swing!"

The president of the United States of America picked up his son and began to swing him as they moved down the hall.

"*Whhhheeeeeeeee!!!!!*" they both exclaimed.

16

Late that night, as Kathryn slept, Thomas, still in his suit but sans tie and coat, sat at the desk in their bedroom, reading briefs, news accounts, and letters. Despite the day's sense of resolution, he knew nothing had ended. Planets would still orbit; suns and galaxies would still revolve; the universe would continue to expand. Closer to home, life would continue; business would still need to be attended to; the nation's governance was unending. Still, he could not help feeling that all that would now happen with a slightly different tone. He both relaxed in a pleasant anticipation of what that meant and sat on the edge of his seat in apprehension—a dichotomy not unusual in politics, government, or life.

"*Psst! Hey! Thomas!*"

It was the slightest of whispers and the loudest of shouts—another dichotomy.

"Oh, no," Thomas whispered. He had convinced himself that it had all been a dream. Or a series of dreams. Or a series of psychotic interludes. But it did not matter as the effect of everything he was happy with.

"*Come here.*"

"And where might 'here' be?" Thomas said to nothing but space in front of him.

"*The Lincoln Bedroom.*"

Knowing it would be useless to do anything but comply, Thomas got up, left his bedroom, entered the West Sitting Hall, left that comfortable room, and walked down the center hall to the Lincoln Bedroom. Entering, he found Tommy, his homunculus, the size again of a child, in a tee-shirt and shorts, impishly bouncing on the famous, revered, cherished, ornate rosewood, eight-foot-long Lincoln bed. Jumping as high as the room's chandelier and shooting rubber bands at it each time he reached its level.

"Hey! Look at me!"

"Would you cut that out!

Tommy continued to bounce. "Why? You're going to let Charlie."

"Charlie is my son."

"And I'm your...?"

"Worst—" But he could not say it. Of course, he could not. For it was simply not true. "No, *best* nightmare."

Tommy stopped in mid-bounce and gently floated down to the bed. "Well, I'm glad you can finally see that."

But that solved no riddle; it answered no question.

"Who—or what—or who are you?"

Tommy took a contemplative stance—not easy on a bed—bringing his hand to his chin and concentration to his brow. "Hmmm—I don't know. I could be a hallucination, I suppose, but I don't think you've dropped acid or eaten some funny mushrooms lately, right? I could be a *fig*—" Tommy held out his right palm, and upon it was some fruit from the *Ficus carica* tree "—*mint* of your imagination." And in his left palm, now also held out, was a small white, sparkling tablet. "Get it? *Fig*—" He held out his right palm. "*Mint!*" And then his left palm and looked at Thomas in anticipation of hilarity striking him.

But Thomas was unmoved to laughter. A little affectionate smile, however, did appear on his lips.

"No," the imp said, "it couldn't have been that. Because, before today, you didn't have any imagination! Of course, you could be certifiable, and I could be a delusion, but that would not bode well for the country, would it? Freud could have been right, and I could be your Id or the devil on your shoulder!" Tommy burst into flames, at the core of which was his devil self, laughing maniacally. But the fire, after illuminating the Victorian yellow wallpaper surrounding, extinguished quickly, leaving the impish but still slightly maniacal Tommy behind, a big, wicked smile stretching across his face.

He prepped himself for a big bounce and then took it. It was not a straight-up bounce but one with a high arc and trajectory that landed him on the floor before Thomas.

As Tommy stood straight, he morphed into a tall, rail-thin man dressed in a black frock coat, waistcoat, trousers, tie, and stovepipe top hat. His worn, craggy, bearded face turned its melancholy, yet somehow warm and loving, eyes upon Thomas. "Or I just might be," the apparition said with an unmistakable, tenor twang, "the better angel of your nature."

Thomas took a breath through a dropped mouth and held it as he stared at the six-foot-four man before him. The apparition held out a large hand, and Thomas took it. It engulfed his own and was warm and fleshy.

"Goodbye, Tom," the apparition said in a sweet voice and slowly faded from the room.

Kathryn had awoken and, missing her husband, went looking for him and found him standing in the middle of the Lincoln Bedroom with his right arm extended.

"Honey, what are you doing in here?"

"Oh, uh, well, I like to come in here sometimes during quiet moments."

"You know, so do I."

"Really?"

"Yes."

"Wow."

Thomas looked around the room, now a bedroom but once Lincoln's office, where he signed the Emancipation Proclamation. There, so much tortured contemplation, deep fears, unbounded courage, and difficult decisions still clung to the walls.

Kathryn wanted to return Thomas to their room; she knew he must be exhausted. But she could feel his reluctance to leave. And so, she thought, why should he? "Honey?"

"Yes?"

"Would you like to sleep here tonight?"

"Could I?"

"Well, of course, Honey. You're the president of the United States."

"Oh, yeah. Okay. I'll go get my pajamas."

Kathryn walked up to him and placed an open hand on his chest. "Uh, later, get your pajamas later." Then her hand went to his cheek and her lips to his lips.

President Thomas P. Powell was elected to his first full term with a comfortable majority two years later.

The End

ABOUT THE AUTHOR

Photo by Amanda Martin

Before publishing twelve critically acclaimed works of fiction, award-winning and Amazon bestselling author Steven Paul Leiva spent over twenty years in the entertainment industry as a writer and producer. He worked with such talent as Academy Award-winning producer Richard Zanuck; director Ivan Reitman; literary legend and screenwriter Ray Bradbury; *Star Wars* producer Gary Kurtz; Looney Tunes legend Chuck Jones; and Animation Feature Academy Award-winning director Brad Bird. He even lent his voice to the Academy Award shortlisted (placing in the top ten) animated short, "The Indescribable Nth."

Leiva produced the animation for the original *Space Jam,*

starring the very tall Michael Jordan and the relatively short Bugs Bunny. For this production, Leiva put together an ad hoc animation studio for Warner Bros and executive producer Ivan Reitman in three days over the phone.

During this time, he wrote novels and a play *Made on the Moon*, which premiered at the Edinburgh Festival Fringe, receiving a four-star review from *The Scotsman*.

After *Space Jam*, Leiva decided to concentrate on writing novels. Since 2003, he has published eleven novels, a novella, and a book of essays.

His work has been praised by literary great Ray Bradbury, Oscar-winning film producer Richard Zanuck, *New York Times* bestselling author and Pulitzer Prize finalist Diane Ackerman, *New York Times* Bestselling Author Jonathan Maberry, comedy great Phil Proctor of The Firesign Theater, *USA Today* Bestselling Author Jean Rabe, *Star Trek: Enterprise* actor John Billingsley, Australian philosopher Russell Blackford, and British physicist and author Stephen Webb. He has received the Scribe Award from the International Association of Media Tie-in Writers.

You can learn more about Steven Paul Leiva on his blog at https://emotionalrationalist.blogspot.com/

BOOKS BY STEVEN PAUL LEIVA

Blood is Pretty: The First Fixxer Adventure

Meet the Fixxer—with wit and aplomb, he works the fruitful fields of Hollywood, fixing the sins and correcting the stupidities of the denizens therein. In *Blood is Pretty* he comes to the rescue of "the most beautiful woman I have ever seen" to extricate her from the grip of the soul-sucking sexual desires of a producer born in slime, and takes on the task of buying off with money and muscle a film geek who won't cooperate with a director of minuscule talent who simply wants to claim "V"—the geek's "Holy Grail" of a film treatment—as his own.

Hollywood is an All-Volunteer Army: The Second Fixxer Adventure

What those in the know in Hollywood really know is that if they need a dark deed done, if they need a sticky personal or professional problem "fixed," they can call upon the mysterious and dangerous Fixxer. Whether you are a successful comedy film director whose "Art" has never truly been appreciated because the country's most important film critic has held a grudge against you since college or you are a neophyte and naïve screenwriter who resents the professional blackmail she has just suffered, you call upon the Fixxer.

Traveling in Space

A unique first contact novel from the aliens' point-of-view.
International Amazon First Contact SF Bestseller

The last thing the factfinders—who call themselves Life—expected to find while traveling in space in "The Curious" on a mission from their planet, The Living World, was other life. But one day, they stumble upon the third planet out from a backwater sun and find it teeming with a vast diversity of life, including one sentient and cognizant, if primitive, species that they dub Otherlife. Being not only from The Curious but inherently curious themselves, they begin to study the Otherlife and their alien culture, discovering such strange things as marriage, intoxicating drinks, weapons of minor and mass destruction, the gleeful inhaling of toxic substances, two-parent families, layered language, genocide, non-nude bathing, and—the strangest thing of all—religion.

This first contact between Life and Otherlife, disconcerting for both, has moments of humor and moments of horror—and neither escape the encounter unchanged.

12 Dogs of Christmas
A Novelization

Winner of the Scribe Award from the International Association of Media Tie-in Authors
Based on the beloved independent family film.

12-year-old Emma O'Connor is sent to live with her "aunt" in the small town of Doverville. Emma soon finds herself in the middle of a "dogfight" with the mayor and town dogcatcher. In order to strike down their "no-dogs" law, Emma must bring together a group of schoolmates, grown-ups, and adorable dogs of all shapes and sizes in a spectacular holiday pageant. *The 12 Dogs of Christmas* is a fun, heartwarming story featuring a diverse canine cast and is perfect for all those who love dogs, kids, and Christmas.

By the Sea
A Comic Novel

A modern comic adult fairy tale with an ensemble cast of Cinderellas. Instead of a kingdom by the sea, our story takes place in and around a residential hotel by the sea. The architecturally eclectic Briers Hotel is situated on Leech Beach, a not particularly inviting beach that is often fog-bound and always scruffy. But it's the perfect setting for our Cinderellas, male, and female, who put up with the scruffiness of life while striving to make it through their various personal seaside fogs. Theater; art; antiques; old movies; sex; more sex; death; fast and slow cars, chicken shit, and cow poop; military bearing and erotic emissions—not to mention the wicked witch, the sea serpent by the sea shore, the village ogre, the village idiot, and several Prince Charmings—all figure into this merry tale with a multitude of happy endings.

IMP
A Political Fantasia

Thomas P. Powell's ascension in politics was both unusual and yet very American. From traffic cop to Vice President of the United States, his climb up the ladder of public service was often due to the push of random acts and not-so-happy accidents—although Thomas held the opinion that it was due solely to his singular innate moral authority. What matters is what's within, that's the Powell political philosophy. Then, on the cusp of his grasping the last rung of the American political ladder, something truly within suddenly appears. A horrible homunculus, an impetuous imp, climbs out of Thomas's right ear to bedevil his nights, confuse his days, and take him on a crazy, wild, nauseating, and nuclear journey. It's as if *The West Wing* was done as a *Twilight Zone* episode.

And you thought our last political nightmare was surreal.

Journey to Where
A Contemporary Scientific Romance
International Amazon Science Fiction Bestseller

When a radical experiment into the nature of time is sabotaged, the scientific team finds themselves in an alternate universe where humans never became the dominant life force. Instead, dinosaurs evolved into intelligent bipeds, developing language and societal structures.

The scientists must learn to communicate with this alien species, who view them as unusual pets, and figure out how to recreate the original experiment in a non-industrialized world so they can go back home—assuming there's a home, or even a universe, to return to. But the scientist who sabotaged them is trapped in this new world with them. And he's looking to rise to power, even if his quest means the death of his traveling companions.

A contemporary scientific romance in the tradition of H. G. Wells and Jules Verne

Creature Feature
A Horrid Comedy

Named a "TOP BOOK OF 2020" by the Montreal Times!
Amazon International Bestseller
Amazon #1 Political Humor Bestseller

THERE IS SOMETHING STRANGE HAPPENING IN PLACIDVILLE!

It is 1962. Kathy Anderson, a serious actress who took her training at the Actors Studio in New York is stuck playing Vivacia, the Vampire Woman on *Vivacia's House of Horrors* for a local Chicago TV station. Finally fed up showing old monster movies to creature feature fans, she quits and heads to New York, and the fame and footlights of Broadway.

Kathy stops off to visit her parents and old friends in Placidville, the all-American, middle-class, blissfully normal Midwest small town she grew up in. But she finds things are strange in Placidville. Kathy's parents, her best friend from high school, the local druggist, and even the Oberhausen twins are all acting curiously creepy, odiously odd, and wholly weird. Especially the town's super geeky nerd, Gerald, who warns of dark days ahead.

Has Kathy entered a zone in the twilight? Did she reach the limits that are outer? Has she fallen through a mirror that is black? Or is it just—just—politics as usual?

The Definition of Luck
Or
The Post-Modern Prometheus

A work of contrarian science fiction? You decide.

Khadambi Kinyanjui, a 6-foot-five Kenyan who grew up in London, is from a wealthy family. Joe Smith, quite a bit shorter, is a red-headed orphan who grew up with his Aunt Liz in a hole in the California desert. Both are brilliant scientists. One is a neurobiologist, the other an astronomer, who first meet in 2049 under the Tommy Trojan statue at the University of Southern California. They become the best of friends but a very odd couple. And yet, their brotherhood is more robust than most actual brothers.

Then tragedy strikes the pair. Death is near for one of them. What can fend it off? Can the mind, the *self*, be uploaded to some digital realm? Can one become more than a human and far less than an animal? Or will the fix be something unexpected and mysterious? Can this human survive? Can humanity? Can friendship?

Bully 4 Love
A Rather Odd Love Story

NAMED A "FAVORITE BOOK OF 2021" BY THE MONTREAL TIMES!

Adolphus Seruya is a happy, middle-aged, unambitious bachelor and a history professor at a prominent community college. Then suddenly SHE walks into his classroom. Lavinia Carson is beautiful in a unique and compelling way. And radiant almost beyond description. Thus begins a rather odd story of love rejected, love ignored, love found—and cuttlefish pizza.

Extraordinary Voyages

What if a man wanted to go to the moon from the time he was an infant? Not a toddler, not a child, not a young man, but a babe in his mother's arms?

What if Baron Munchausen traveled from 1790 to1641 to take Cyrano de Bergerac to Mars?

What if the man who wanted to go to the moon from the time he was an infant wrote some rude poems?

What if the author of this book wrote his own Wikipedia page that he was sure Wikipedia would never publish?

What if you bought this book and found out?

Includes the critically acclaimed novella *Made on the Moon.*

The Reluctant Heterosexual
A Tragicomedy in Four Movements a Prelude and an Interlude

With *The Reluctant Heterosexual,* Steven Paul Leiva concludes his thematic trilogy: **The Love, Sex and Pursuit of Happiness Novels**. All three novels look at these essential aspects of the human condition, with each novel focusing on one of the three. *By the Sea: A Comic Novel* looks at our unease when unhappy. *Bully 4 Love: A Rather Odd Love Story* takes a skewed view of this most revered emotion. And now, *The Reluctant Heterosexual,* as the title predicts, concerns sex, which is not always the same as love, nor is it always a happy situation.

Subtitled *A Tragicomedy in Four Movements a Prelude and an Interlude,* each section of the novel, as in a musical composition, has its own tempo, mood, and form as it tells the story—and stories—of Robert Leslie Cromwell and Sandy Smith. Two *Homo sapiens sapiens* surviving and striving in the late 20th century.

Robert and Sandy are intelligent, creative, not unattractive, wealthy, married to each other, and in love. And yet their procreating bodies might as well be standing naked on a savanna in Africa in the late Pliocene Era.

It's the sometimes comic conflict between ancient bodies and modern culture. Can there possibly be a happy ending?

Right
A Portrait of Controversy

In a 1980s America different from our own, both familiar and not, Congress passed and President Henshaw signed the Birth Cessation

Act. Once it became law, no one would be allowed to have a child for twenty-five years, any woman under 24 weeks pregnant was required to have an immediate abortion, and all men were called up to report for a vasectomy.

"Conscious regulation of human numbers must be achieved." Dr. Paul R. Ehrlich wrote in his 1968 bestseller, *The Population Bomb*. By the early 80s, the government had statistical projections that the population growth was outpacing the available resources needed for all in America to live a comfortable and secure life. A situation that would inevitably lead to the chaos and violence of extreme civil unrest.

Most Americans, liking comfort and security, supported the government's action. Most, but not all. And those who didn't, including a world-famous female billionaire entrepreneur inventor film producer, a major appliance salesman from Queens, a well-to-do Manhattan college radical, an unwed mother in Los Angeles who protests most horribly, America's premier pundit-columnist, and a young man who talks to his dead brother, became loud enough to start a fresh new controversy in America.

This is a portrait of that controversy.

Searching for Ray Bradbury
Writings about the Writer and
the Man

Includes the title piece written for the *Los Angeles Times*, and "The Man Who Was Himself," Leiva's memorial appreciation of Bradbury commissioned by the Science Fiction & Fantasy Writers of America for the Winter 2012/13 edition of their quarterly magazine, *The Bulletin*. Other pieces were originally written for *Neworld Review*, KCET.org, and his personal blog.

With a special foreword by Hugo and Nebula Award-winning author David Brin.

IMP